Holly's Hometown Heartache

STASIA DIANN

STAZ

Contents

Prologue

Holly's life was just fine, or so she thought. Working as a law clerk for a fast-paced legal firm in Chicago while studying for the bar exam left little time for socializing, especially long-term relationships. So what if she barely dated, and when she did, it was often either awkward or ended in disaster? She couldn't quite admit to herself that she'd never gotten over her high school boyfriend. But the family tragedy that was about to occur will force her to spend several weeks in her small hometown. It will also force her to face another heartache that she's never really come to terms with.

Chapter One

Holly had been in the middle of a deep sleep when the phone rang. Between her demanding job as a law clerk and studying to take the bar exam, she was usually exhausted at the end of each day and needed every minute of sleep she could get.

Still groggy, she fumbled for the phone on the dresser next to the bed. When she saw it was her brother, Hank, she was suddenly wide awake. She rarely heard from Hank these days. Holly couldn't even remember the last time she'd spoken to him.

"Hello," she said nervously.

"Holly, it's Hank. I don't know what time it is in Chicago, but I'm assuming it's pretty late."

"It's the middle of the night. What's going on? Are you in some kind of trouble?"

For as long as she could remember, Hank had been struggling with one problem after another. The last she'd heard, he was living in Los Angeles, trying to break into acting.

"It's not me," Hank insisted. "It's Mom and Dad."

Holly was now out of bed and pacing the floor in her small apartment. "What about Mom and Dad?"

"This isn't going to be easy, so I'll just come out and say it. Mom and Dad were in a car wreck. It was bad. Dad didn't make it, and Mom is in intensive care."

Holly fell back, thankful the bed was still behind her. She sat there for a few seconds, stunned by such devastating news.

"Holly? Are you still there?"

"Yes, Hank, I'm still here. When did this happen? Are you back home in Sandalwood?"

"No, I'm in Los Angeles. Apparently, my name and number are still on paperwork regarding the restaurant. Anyway, the police just called me and said the accident occurred earlier tonight. That's all I know," he said, barely above a whisper. Hank was not one to get emotional about much of anything. But his voice was cracking, and he could barely speak.

Holly took several deep breaths to calm herself. "I'll get home as soon as I can," she said, still holding back the tears. "Hank, are you coming home?"

There was an uncomfortable silence before Hank finally said, "Yeah, I'll get there as soon as I can."

Holly put down the phone and stared out over the city lights. Maybe this was a nightmare, and when she woke up, life would go on like it always did. She could feel her heart pounding in her chest, and her hand hurt from gripping the phone so tightly. This was all too real.

She dropped to her knees at the edge of the bed and said a prayer.

Dear Lord, What is happening... Why is this happening?

Even in her head, these were the only words she could form. All she could do for the next several minutes was breathe, and even that was slow and labored.

She glanced at the clock. It was almost three. It was no use trying to get any more sleep tonight. She needed to take a shower and try to get either plane tickets or a car rental to Ohio.

By nine that morning, she'd found a flight out of O'Hare that would take her to Columbus, Ohio, later that day. From Columbus, she'd rent a car and make the hour drive to her hometown of Sandalwood, Ohio.

After her travel plans were confirmed, she called Sherman and Oaks Law Firm and informed her boss that she would be out of the office for at least a week.

"Take all the time you need," Lora said.

Holly grabbed a suitcase from the back of the closet and began to pack. While mindlessly stuffing her suitcase, a thousand thoughts swirled through her mind at once.

Her dad, not even sixty yet, was gone instantly in a car wreck, and her mom, Caroline, who had been married to Joseph Bennett for over thirty years, was in intensive care in the hospital. They were a kind, hard-working couple. Holly couldn't wrap her head around why this had happened to her mom and dad. When she couldn't bear thinking of her parents any longer, her mind wandered to the people and places she so seldom thought of anymore.

Faces from the past, from the small town in Ohio she'd grown up in yet left behind years ago, filled her thoughts. Sure, she came home a few times a year to visit her parents, usually at Christmas and once during the summer, but she spent the entire time at the house and never went into town. Her parents usually came to Chicago a few times a year to see her. It was a good arrangement, and Holly didn't see the need to interact with anyone else from Sandalwood.

Of course, she kept in touch with her best friend from high school, Tamron. Holly didn't see her very often, but they did occasionally text and email, keeping up with each other's lives.

Tamron had chosen a totally different path in life. She had gotten married right out of high school, had a couple of kids, and was a stay-at-home mom. Holly had left for college and a career in the big city. She smiled when thinking of what a great friend Tamron had always been.

But then she thought about Andrew. Andrew Preston was the primary reason she had left Sandalwood, Ohio, rarely to return. While not necessarily ugly, the breakup had been awkward and confusing. And it had hurt a lot more than she thought it would, even after all these years.

She sometimes wondered how her life would have turned out if they had stayed together. They had been a couple during their junior and senior years in high school. They were both eighteen, barely out of high school, and each was going in different directions in life when they broke up.

Holly continued to mindlessly stuff the suitcase full of clothes while trying to push thoughts of Andrew out of her mind. That had been eight long years ago, and even if she saw him again, it would be no big deal. She tried to convince herself of that as she closed the suitcase and walked out of her apartment.

The last she'd heard, Andrew was engaged to Penelope Gables. Penelope had been in the class two years after them in high school. Penelope had been a giggly blonde, and she was surprised that she and Andrew had gotten together at all.

Holly was tall and thin and had long auburn hair. She'd never pictured Andrew going for someone like Penelope and had been surprised, to say the least, when she'd heard about their engagement a few years earlier. They were almost certainly married by now, and she wondered if they had any kids yet.

She knew she needed to get Andrew Preston out of her head. On the other hand, he was the only thing that could even temporarily help her from constantly dwelling on the fact that her dad was gone and her mother was in the hospital.

On her way to O'Hare Airport, she called the Sandalwood Community Hospital. They wouldn't give her much information over the phone, only that her mother's condition had stabilized since she'd been brought in.

The flight from Chicago to Columbus was relatively short and uneventful. About a half hour into the flight, she suddenly realized she'd barely shed a tear since Hank had called several hours earlier. She wasn't sure if it was because she was still in shock or if she was simply burying all the emotion for the time being. She was traveling, sitting in the middle of a plane, and focusing on getting from Chicago to Sandalwood. She couldn't allow herself to break down yet.

Maybe her love life, or lack thereof, was something mindless and safe to think about. The truth was, she didn't have time to date or invest in a relationship, and the few times she had tried, it had been disappointing, to say the least. And often not just disappointing, but awkward.

There had been Curt, the guy she'd met at the gym. There had just been no chemistry in that relationship. Kissing Curt had felt like kissing her brother. After a few months of infrequent dates, that had fizzled out.

After Curt, there had been Joaquin, a personal trainer and aspiring male model who had also been the brother of her former boss. When Holly found out he was a casual drug user, she knew he wasn't the right guy for her. But Holly had never been good at breakups and continued to see him long after it was apparent that the relationship wasn't going anywhere.

There had been a few other guys, here and there, but nothing that would turn into a serious, long-term relationship. Holly wanted to get married and have a family. Even though she loved living in the city, it was hard to find someone who shared her faith and values. Maybe it just wasn't meant to be, not yet anyway.

Suddenly, a bout of turbulence caused her to forget about awkward kisses and relationships that went nowhere. A few seconds later, the pilot announced that they would be landing in Columbus soon.

As soon as Holly was off the plane and heading to pick up her luggage, she saw a text from Hank.

I'm borrowing a friend's van. I should be in Sandalwood in a few days.

Holly stared at the text in disbelief. He was borrowing a friend's car and was driving from California to Ohio? If this was a leisurely visit, she might understand, but their dad had just died, and their mother was in the hospital.

Financially, Hank must have been in a pretty bad place if he couldn't afford an airline ticket or a rental car during a family emergency.

Holly quickly texted back that she'd buy him a ticket so he could fly. After several minutes passed without hearing anything, she called and left a message. Either he wasn't checking his phone, or he was simply too proud to accept her offer of help. Holly stuffed the phone back in her purse and headed toward the rental car desk.

It was late afternoon by the time Holly drove past the *Welcome to Sandalwood* sign on the outskirts of town. There were maybe a dozen cars lined up at the first stoplight. This was rush hour in Sandalwood.

There would be four more stoplights and one left turn before arriving at the hospital.

At the second stoplight, a few more cars joined the afternoon traffic jam. This gave Holly a few minutes to look around and take in all the sights of downtown.

From what she could remember, absolutely nothing had changed. The barbershop, the drugstore, and the car wash were all exactly as she had remembered them. Then she caught sight of Jack's Ice Cream Shoppe, and the tears started to flow. Her dad had taken Holly and Hank to get ice cream nearly every Sunday afternoon after church when they were kids.

The shock of losing her father had subsided, and the reality had finally hit. By the time she found a parking spot near the hospital, Holly had been crying for several minutes.

Taking a deep breath, she reached for some tissues in her purse. She reapplied her makeup, brushed her long hair, and headed for the hospital entrance.

Chapter Two

It had been years since Holly had been to the Sandalwood Community Hospital. But she immediately recognized the front lobby. Holly was certain the paint on the walls and the carpeting were still the same from the last time she'd been there. She'd sprained her ankle during her senior year, and she vividly remembered Hank and her dad helping her from the car to the information desk.

As Holly waited, several women in cubicles casually chatted as if they had all the time in the world. Finally, a woman in scrubs stood up and forced a weak smile. "Can I help you?"

"I'm here to see Caroline Bennett. Can you tell me what room she's in?"

"I'll have to see if your name is on the list," the nurse said crisply.

"I'm her daughter!" Holly said, nearly shouting.

The nurse narrowed her eyes. "You're Holly? Why, I haven't seen you since you were in high school."

Even in her sleep-deprived state, Holly suddenly remembered Virginia James.

"Yes, I'm Holly. I'm sorry I yelled at you."

Virginia reached out and touched Holly's arm. "It's okay. I'm so sorry for everything that's happened. Your mother is in room 234."

"Thank you," Holly said softly. She kept forgetting she was back in a small town, where everyone pretty much knew everyone else.

When the elevator door opened, she hesitantly stepped out into the hall. The second floor was quiet, with only the sound of a few nurses talking at the desk. They ignored Holly as she scanned the numbers over the tops of the doors.

Holly couldn't wait to see her mother, yet dreaded seeing her in this condition. Both of her parents had always been so healthy.

When she found room 234, Holly stopped and said a quick prayer, asking for the grace to be able to deal with whatever she was about to encounter.

She pushed open the door and let out a gasp. The entire left side of her mom's face was bandaged, both legs were bandaged, and her left arm was in a cast.

"Mom," she whispered.

The right side of Caroline Bennett's face curved up into a slight smile. Her right arm, the only part of her body that wasn't bruised or bandaged, reached out for her daughter.

"Oh, Mom!" Holly broke down again and cried while holding her mom's hand.

"I'm actually not as bad as I look," she said softly. "I don't know if they told you, but..."

"I know. Dad didn't make it," Holly said, the tears streaming down her face.

Her mother looked away. Her eyes were swollen, and her voice was groggy. Between the physical pain and the medication she was likely on, Holly didn't know how much of her dad's death her mother was processing at this point. Holly was at a loss for words and just held her mother's hand.

After a few minutes, Holly gently asked about the accident. "How did it all happen?"

Mom took several labored breaths before answering. "We were coming home from dinner at the Felger's, and the bridge over Coleman Creek went out." She squeezed her eyes shut, remembering the fateful moment the bridge crumbled beneath them.

Holly took a second to process what she was hearing. The creek was only a few feet deep, especially in the fall. But there was a steep embankment, and if they were near the middle of the bridge, it would have been at least a twenty-foot drop.

She was about to ask if Mom had been conscious during the accident when she heard footsteps. Without letting go of her mother's hand, she turned to see a petite woman in dark blue scrubs.

"Are you Mrs. Bennett's daughter?"

Holly nodded.

"I'm Bridget, her nurse. We're glad you're here. She's been asking about you all day."

Holly turned back around and saw her mom's eyes fluttering and then gently closing. Holly sat next to her for several minutes, holding her hand and listening to her strained breathing.

When the nurse said it was time to check her vitals and change her IV, Holly stepped out to get some coffee. She managed to find her way to the cafeteria and make her way back in about fifteen minutes.

When Holly got back to the room, she was pleasantly surprised to see her old friend Tamron Johnson sitting at her mother's bedside.

"Tamron!" Holly cried.

Tamron stood up and embraced her dear friend. "I'm so sorry about your dad," she said.

"Thanks," Holly said, fighting the urge to cry again.

"Why don't you two take a break and catch up?" Mom said softly.

"Mom, I hate to leave you. I just got back."

"I'm really tired. You go ahead."

"All right," Holly said. "I'll be back to check on you before too long."

"Let me buy you dinner in the cafeteria," Tamron said eagerly. "We've got a lot of catching up to do."

Once in the cafeteria, they ordered chicken sandwiches and iced tea and proceeded to find a small table in the back where it was quiet.

"So, how have you been?" Holly asked while unwrapping her sandwich.

"Pretty much the same as always. Matt is still at the same job, Marcus is in preschool now, and both my parents are doing well." Tamron suddenly felt a wave of guilt after nonchalantly saying her parents were fine after what had happened to Holly's parents. "I'm sorry, Holly. I wasn't even thinking."

Holly shook her head. "That's okay. I want to know what's going on with everyone. It will help keep my mind occupied."

Tamron smiled and pushed her curly blonde hair behind her ears. "Everyone and everything pretty much stays the same here. You know that."

"After eight years, how many people from our class are married?" Holly asked. She wanted to change the subject so she could take her mind off the fact that she'd just lost her dad.

"I'd say almost half. You know, people in a small town seem to marry younger than those living in the big city."

Holly nodded. "Yeah, most of my friends and colleagues in Chicago are still single."

Tamron started naming several of their classmates who were married and those who had children. When Holly realized she hadn't mentioned Andrew, she gently interrupted. "Aren't you forgetting someone?"

Tamron squinted, as if she were in deep thought. "I don't think so. Who are you thinking of?"

"You're going to make me say it? Isn't Andrew Preston married to Penelope Gables?"

Tamron suddenly had a really awkward look on her face. "Obviously, you never heard what happened."

"What happened? Did something bad happen to Andrew?" Holly even surprised herself by how concerned she was.

"Nothing bad, unless you consider breaking his engagement to Penelope bad."

Now, Holly was the one who wasn't sure what to say. "I can't believe no one told me. When did this happen? The last time I heard anything about Andrew was when Mom told me he'd gotten engaged."

"They'd been engaged for several months. In fact, Andrew broke it off less than a month before the wedding. I guess it's been about a year since all that happened," Tamron said.

"Why did he break up with her?" Holly asked, trying not to sound too interested.

"That's the big mystery. No one really ever knew. They pretty much kept it between themselves."

"That's strange," Holly said. "Is Andrew still living in Sandalwood?"

"Yeah, he's an accountant. He works downtown."

After that, Tamron told Holly everything else that was happening in Sandalwood while they finished their sandwiches. Holly would later realize she didn't remember any of it. She couldn't take her mind off the fact that Andrew hadn't married Penelope and was still single.

***

After Tamron left, Holly spent the rest of the evening with her mom. The doctor had upgraded her condition and told Holly he believed she would make a full recovery with time.

When Mom woke, revived from her nap, she didn't seem concerned for herself but for Holly.

"Holly, you look exhausted. You should go back to the house and get some rest. The key is under the plant by the front door."

Holly almost laughed. She'd forgotten how people in Sandalwood still hid their keys on the front porch. "Mom, you're my priority right now. This is where I want to be."

"If you really want to help me, make sure the restaurant is doing okay."

"I thought you said Gary and Eileen were taking care of things."

The last time Mom had talked about the restaurant, she'd raved about their short-order cook, Gary Noles, and how his wife, Eileen, was basically managing the place while she and Dad were taking more time off and starting to ease into retirement.

"Yes, they've been doing more of the daily tasks, but your dad and I were still involved and went in several times a week."

"I'll check in tomorrow and see how they're doing," Holly reassured her mom.

"Have you heard from Hank?" Mom asked.

"Yes, he's on his way."

Mom nodded her head, thankful he was coming to see her. She didn't ask when Hank was expected, and Holly didn't volunteer the information. Unless Mom asked how he was getting here, there was no need to tell her that Hank was driving a friend's van across the country.

"Really, you should go home and get some rest," Mom insisted.

Holly finally agreed. Even though she wanted to ask Mom why no one had told her about Andrew's broken engagement, she knew now wasn't the time.

Chapter Three

Holly woke the next morning groggy and, for a moment, unsure of where she was. So much had happened during the last twenty-four hours. The moment the memories all came flooding into her brain, she let out an exasperated sigh. The fact that her dad was gone and her mother was in the hospital hit her like a brick wall.

"Just get up and keep moving," she whispered to herself.

Her childhood home was so lonely and quiet when she was the only one there. She had so many fond memories growing up in a traditional colonial-style home at the end of Oak Street. They were part of a neighborhood, yet far enough at the very end of the street that the house was secluded. The fact that several large leafy trees separated their home from the next offered even more privacy.

As she dressed and headed downstairs to make a cup of instant coffee, she remembered racing her baby brother Henry down the steps so many mornings during her childhood. Only a few years apart, they had been so close while growing up.

They had talked about everything back then. Their childhood dreams, their hopes for the future, and even their romantic interests. Hank, as he preferred to be called once they got to high school, hadn't been that wild about any of her boyfriends until she started seeing Andrew.

Holly shook her head in frustration, thinking how so many memories always seemed to find their way back to Andrew. The microwave beeped, and she pulled out her steaming cup of coffee.

Sitting at the table, she scrolled through her phone, looking for a familiar passage of Scripture.

Psalm 46:10. *Be still and know that I am God.*

Holly had a busy day ahead of her. This verse was simple but just what she needed this morning. After reading all of Psalm 46 and finishing most of her coffee, she was ready to start her day.

First, she'd visit her mom and see what sort of plans needed to be made for her rehab. Then she needed to meet with Pastor Hawkins to start planning her dad's funeral. Sometime in the afternoon, she'd have to log onto her computer, get some work done, and connect with her boss. She'd also have to stop by the restaurant and make sure everything was running smoothly there.

Maybe she'd have lunch at the restaurant. That way, she could find out how things were going while also finding time to eat a decent meal. There wasn't much food in the fridge, and she didn't have time to do grocery shopping.

Holly scrolled through her phone to see if there was anything from Hank yet. Nothing.

She was torn between worrying about her brother and being angry that he was leaving her to handle everything here on her own. They had both left Sandalwood for different reasons, but he had been the black sheep of the family, while she had always been the good girl.

She looked down at the Bible verse again. With a renewed sense of strength, Holly headed out the front door to start her day.

It took less than ten minutes to drive from the house to the hospital, park the car, and get inside. This was definitely one thing she didn't miss about Chicago: how long it often took just to run a simple errand.

Mom was alert and doing better than expected at the hospital.

"Your mother has really improved during the last 24 hours," the doctor said after making his morning rounds.

"That's wonderful," Holly said, smiling at Mom. "What are the next steps in her recovery process?"

"I'm going to order physical therapy to start today," he said eagerly.

Holly glanced at her mom, still covered in both bandages and bruises. "This soon?" she said, giving the doctor an unapproving look.

The doctor adamantly nodded his head. "She needs to start regaining muscle function and mobility as soon as possible. Therapy will also help reduce inflammation and pain."

Mom rested her hand on Holly's arm. "I'm ready," she said firmly. "I'm already tired of sitting in this bed all day."

Holly reluctantly agreed, realizing how active her mom had always been.

When Mom started talking about Dad and the funeral, Holly didn't add much to the conversation. She still wasn't ready to accept his death, and discussing the funeral made her uncomfortable.

She thought about bringing up Hank and asking if he had texted or called Mom. But that made her almost as uneasy. Besides, what if he hadn't called or texted since the accident? Holly was also still upset that her mom hadn't told her about Andrew's broken engagement. But with the doctor and a nurse still hovering in the room, she didn't feel comfortable bringing it up. The only other thing she could currently think of was the restaurant.

"I'm going to stop by the diner in a little bit. Is there anything in particular you want me to check on?" Holly asked.

Mom started running through a laundry list of things she wanted Holly to look into to make sure everything was running as smoothly as possible. Holly was thankful she'd changed the subject. But at the end of the list was a request for her to stop by the church and meet with Pastor Hawkins regarding Dad's funeral.

Holly sighed. "Sure, Mom. I'll take care of everything."

***

Even though Holly had contacted the church before leaving the hospital, Pastor Hawkins had been called to an emergency meeting and was not in his office when Holly arrived. At this point, it was after eleven, and she decided to swing by the restaurant.

The Bennett Diner had been a staple of life in Sandalwood for over twenty years. Joseph and Caroline Bennett had poured their heart and soul into creating both a menu and an atmosphere that resonated with small-town life.

Gary Noles was the head cook at the diner and did an excellent job. His wife, Eileen, worked out front, seating customers and overseeing the servers. Holly's mom and dad, however, still played a vital role in running the restaurant. They oversaw all the staffing, ordering, inventory, managing the finances, and coming up with new menu items.

Now that Dad had passed away and Mom had injuries that could possibly take months to heal, Holly believed it was time to sell the restaurant. But Mom was so adamant about keeping it going. Holly parked her car in the back and walked around to the front to get a good look at the restaurant.

Bennett's Diner was still in basic black letters across the front. Holly opened the front door and took a good look at the place. Nothing ever changed in Sandalwood.

The lunch crowd was just starting to flow into the restaurant, and it wasn't very busy yet. But a few of the people who were there instantly recognized her. Mr. and Mrs. Krebs, who ran the bakery across the street, stood up and came to greet her. They offered their condolences, and after the customary pleasantries, retreated to their corner booth.

Another elderly lady from church quickly said hello, how good it was to see her again, and how she wished it had been under better circumstances.

When Eileen finally saw Holly and their eyes locked, Holly could no longer hold back the tears. They embraced, and Holly allowed herself to cry briefly. Yes, they were in the middle of a restaurant during business hours, but they were also in a small town among friends. Everyone pretty much knew everyone else. And they all knew the death of Joseph Bennett was a devastating loss to the entire community.

Eileen smiled and gave Holly another quick hug. "It's so good to see you. Would you like something to eat? There are some spots at the counter."

"Maybe in a little bit," Holly said softly. "I told Mom I'd stop by to check on things while she's recovering. I can tell the diner is in very good hands."

"Whenever you're ready, let me know." Eileen patted Holly on the back and then returned to the kitchen.

Holly heard the door open and a gust of wind blow into the diner. She turned around, preparing to meet someone else from town she hadn't seen in years. She definitely saw someone else she hadn't seen in years, but it was the last person she expected.

She was suddenly eye-to-eye with the man who'd broken her heart all those years ago. Andrew Preston still had the same dark, wavy hair and dimpled, boyish grin. But when their eyes locked, the carefree smile left his face. Andrew was obviously just as shocked to run into her.

Chapter Four

Holly was so overwhelmed seeing Andrew after all these years that she was suddenly at a loss for words and momentarily just stared into his large brown eyes.

"Holly, it's been a long time," he said softly.

"Yeah, it has been a long time," was all she could manage.

"I'm so sorry about your dad. I hope your mom gets better quickly."

"Thank you. This has just all been such a shock."

"How long have you been back in town?" he asked, casually folding his arms as if he were settling in for a long conversation.

"I just got back yesterday." She couldn't help but think about how he was even more attractive now that he had physically matured and gotten older. And she felt guilty for thinking things like that, considering the reason she was in town.

"I can't imagine what you're going through," he said, gently reaching out and rubbing her shoulder. "I just came in to grab lunch. I'm sure you're busy, taking care of things here and with your mom."

"Uh, yeah, I am," she said.

Andrew smiled. "If you don't mind me saying, you look exhausted. Why don't you let me buy you lunch? It would be nice to catch up, if you have time."

Holly wanted to say no. Her every instinct just wanted to run out of the diner and not look back. But she was tired and hungry, and something about him caused her to stay. "Sure," she said without thinking. "I do need to sit down and take a break."

"Let's sit over there," he said, pointing to a corner booth.

Holly had only come back to Sandalwood once or twice a year since officially leaving after high school graduation. This was the first time she had seen Andrew face-to-face since the summer after high school. She'd seen a few pictures of him that friends had shown her and photos he'd posted on social media accounts. She wasn't prepared for how she was feeling now that she was seeing him in person again. She tried not to stare as he led the way to a corner booth.

Eileen gave Holly and Andrew a quick side glance and then looked away. Holly knew the gossip would soon be all over town. She pushed all that out of her mind. She'd only be here a week or so, and then she'd be back to her life in Chicago.

Within seconds, the waitress brought two waters and menus. Holly already knew what she wanted, but buried her head in the menu to give herself time to calm down and think. *Breathe deep*, she thought to herself.

"So, how's your mom doing?" Andrew asked.

"As good as can be expected. In fact, since I've been here, she's already improved," Holly said, wondering what in the world he was thinking and wishing she could read his thoughts at that moment. He was acting so casual about seeing her after all these years. Had he just matured into a calm, cool man from the impetuous, high-strung teenager she had known before? Or were every emotion and feeling he'd ever felt for her gone, and was seeing her just like running into any other old friend he'd ever known? Holly couldn't tell, and it irritated her.

"That's great," he said with a warm smile. "What exactly happened? I read news reports that they went over the Coleman Bridge. That bridge has pretty sturdy guardrails."

Holly sighed. "They didn't go through the guardrails. The bridge collapsed." The emotion she felt from reliving what happened to her parents and sitting face-to-face with Andrew was almost too much. But somehow she managed to keep her feelings in check.

Andrew widened his eyes in disbelief. "You're kidding me. You know, I heard several months ago the county was supposed to do some repairs to that bridge. I wonder if they ever did."

"Really? I should look into that," Holly said, trying to process what he'd just said. Even though she couldn't read his emotions or tell how he really felt about her, she was surprised by how comfortable she already felt with him after eight years.

Holly looked back down at the menu. When she looked up again, the waitress was back, ready to take their orders. The diner was starting to get busy, and she didn't look very patient.

Andrew ordered a chicken sandwich with extra pickles and a root beer, and Holly's stomach suddenly twisted in knots. She remembered how he always ordered everything with extra pickles and a root beer. And he still rolled his eyes to one side when he ordered in a restaurant, like he was mulling over some great philosophical debate instead of just ordering lunch.

"I'll take the roast beef special and a cup of coffee," Holly said with a laugh.

"What's so funny?" Andrew said as soon as the waitress left.

"Oh, just that you're still ordering pickles and root beer."

"I guess I have pretty much done that my whole life. Some things never change," he said, giving her the soft, half-smile that had always melted her heart.

"So, what's new in your life?" Holly asked. "Are you still working as an accountant?"

"Yeah, I've been working for the Coburn CPA Group for almost four years now."

Holly nodded, thinking how Coburn was a staple that had been around for dozens of years in Sandalwood, like nearly every other business, including the diner.

Holly chuckled.

"What's so funny now?" Andrew asked.

"In Chicago, new businesses are constantly popping up, and older ones are always closing. That probably doesn't happen very often in Sandalwood."

"No, it doesn't. I can't think of the last time a new business came to town or an old one left. Maybe five years ago, when Mable Owens closed her yogurt shop."

Holly gasped. "Mable Owens had a yogurt shop? For some reason, I can't see that."

"Neither could anyone else. That's probably why it closed."

As they both laughed together, Holly remembered what a great sense of humor Andrew had. She had been attracted to his humor and personality as much as his rugged good looks.

Holly suddenly realized she wasn't nervous anymore. She didn't like that she was already feeling so connected to Andrew again.

"So, do you come to the diner often for lunch?" Holly asked, trying to keep the conversation light.

"Yeah, and a couple of nights in the evening for dinner, too. Being single, I get tired of eating alone every night," he said with a smile. "I'll often sit at the counter just to have some friendly conversation while I'm eating. It's not always easy being single."

"I'd heard you were engaged, but I didn't know until recently that you never got married. I'm sorry," she said, surprising herself that she'd so easily brought up his broken engagement. She hadn't planned on saying that.

"It's okay," he said softly. "Some things just aren't meant to be."

Andrew had a strange look on his face, and Holly wasn't sure if he was just referring to his relationship with Penelope or their relationship years earlier. She was waiting for him to ask if she was married, but, of course, he would have already known if she were. Andrew's mom was in several church groups with Holly's mom. But he didn't even ask if she was seeing anyone else, and she wasn't sure if that upset her or not.

It was the first lull in the conversation, and Holly was thankful when the waitress brought their drinks.

"So, how's Chicago? Do you still like living in the city?" he asked after taking a quick sip of his root beer.

Before Holly had a chance to come up with a response, she felt her phone buzz and looked down to see she had gotten a text from Hank.

I'm at the house. Where are you?

"Oh, my," she said, barely above a whisper.

"Is something wrong?" Andrew said. "Is your mom okay?"

"It's from Hank. He's at the house."

"Your brother, Hank?" Andrew said.

"The one and only," Holly muttered.

"I haven't seen him around. How long has he been back in town?"

"Just now, as far as I know. He drove all the way from California," Holly said, rolling her eyes. "I'm sorry, I'll have to take my lunch to go."

"That's okay," Andrew said. "It sounds like you've got your hands full."

Holly nodded and motioned for the waitress to bring her a carry-out box. For once in her life, she was thankful that Hank had interrupted her. She really didn't know how to feel or act about the fact that Andrew was still single, sitting right in front of her, and they were getting along as if no time at all had passed between them.

"Oh, I need my bill, too," Holly said when the waitress brought her a styrofoam container.

Andrew gently placed his hand over Holly's. "Remember, I said I would get lunch. I'll take care of this."

"Thank you," she said while quickly pulling her hand away. She awkwardly shoved her food into the container.

"Even though I wish it had been under better circumstances, I'm glad I got to see you," Andrew said.

"I am too," she said, sounding more emotional than she hoped to.

Holly grabbed her purse and food and headed out of the diner. She was leaving one emotionally charged situation and heading right into another.

Chapter Five

Hank was sitting on the front porch when Holly arrived back home. The vehicle in the driveway was a rusty van with dents along the left side. This was hardly a rental vehicle, and Holly was surprised he'd even made it from California to Ohio.

Hank stood up and spread his arms as Holly got out of the car and headed toward the porch. "How about a hug for your favorite brother?"

"You're my only brother," she said as she gave him a hug.

He always said that, and she always answered the same way whenever they saw each other, which wasn't very often. Even though Hank had always been the family screw-up, never held a regular job, and even found himself in trouble from time to time, he always had an upbeat, congenial personality that most people were instinctively drawn to.

"I'm not sure how that thing made it from California to Ohio, but I'll be surprised if it makes it back," Holly said, pointing to the dilapidated van.

"I'm not worried. It's got a solid engine. So, how's Mom doing? How's she dealing with Dad's death?"

I'm not worried. Hank's three favorite words.

"As well as can be expected on both counts. Come inside," Holly said. "I'll fix us some coffee before we go see Mom at the hospital. I'll fill you in on everything that's happened."

Holly brewed a pot of coffee and set out a tray of chocolate chip cookies, Hank's favorite since childhood.

She told him about Mom's condition and what was happening at the restaurant while Hank sucked down two cups of coffee and basically inhaled about half a dozen cookies.

Hank was always lanky and thin, but he looked like he'd lost more weight since the last time she'd seen him, which had been a few years.

She poured herself a second cup and told him that the Coleman Bridge had given out, causing the crash into the creek below.

"I always thought that old bridge was rickety and unsafe," he said as he finished off the last of the cookies.

"Andrew just told me the county was supposed to fix that bridge, but he didn't think the repairs were ever finished."

Hank shook his head, as if he were suddenly confused. "Andrew told you? Since when are you seeing Andrew?"

"I am not seeing Andrew," Holly stated indignantly. "I ran into him at the diner. Mom asked me to see how things were going, and he came in for lunch while I was there."

Hank lifted up his hands as if to defend himself. "Okay, okay, just wondering how Andrew suddenly came into the picture."

Holly knew she had protested too much and wanted to quickly change the subject.

"So, what are you doing now out in California?" she asked.

Hank sipped his coffee and smiled. "Oh, working odd jobs and getting some bit roles here and there."

Hank had been fortunate enough to get a few roles as an extra on a handful of low-budget movies, but so far, never a major role.

"Any speaking roles yet?" Holly asked.

"Well, not yet," he said sheepishly. "But I did get a part as one of the neighbors who stood on the sidewalk when a guy's house got blown up in an action movie."

"Hank, how are you paying your bills?"

"I manage," he said, with another big smile.

Holly knew he was either gambling or living on credit cards, but she currently didn't have the motivation to ask him any more questions.

"Come on, let's go see Mom."

***

Mom had been moved to the rehab wing of the hospital, and it took several minutes to find out what room she was in. When Holly and Hank finally got there, they saw Pastor Hawkins sitting by her at the edge of the bed. He immediately stood up and gave them room to gather close to their mom.

Hank finally came close enough to get a good look at the injuries she'd suffered. "Oh, Mom," he said, with more emotion than Holly could ever remember hearing from her brother.

Tears filled Mom's eyes, and she reached out for her son as much as she was able. It had been a long time since Mom had seen Hank. For several seconds, neither said anything while continuing to hug. But as soon as Hank pulled away, Mom got a good look at her son.

"Hank, you look awfully thin," Mom said. "Are you eating regular-ly?"

Holly looked away from both her mom and brother, fearing an argument was about to start even now. Hank wasn't only a big gambler; he'd also been a heavy drinker throughout much of his life. But Hank defused the situation more gracefully than she had anticipated.

"I'm fine, Mom, really. I'm sure Holly will keep me well fed now that I'm here."

"You tell Gary and Eileen you can eat for free," Mom said. "Did you make it to the restaurant yet?"

"Yes, and everything is fine," Holly said quickly before turning and greeting Pastor Hawkins.

"It's so good to see you both. I'm so sorry about your dad." He leaned toward Holly for a hug and then reached out to shake Hank's hand.

Pastor Hawkins was a middle-aged man with a Santa Claus beard and a large waist to match. He had been the pastor of their small non-denominational church since Holly had been in middle school.

"Thank you for being here," Holly said, taking a deep breath to again hold back the tears.

Holly's mom pushed herself up to a sitting position. "We need to start planning your dad's funeral," she said softly.

"It's only been two days since the accident," Holly said. "We've got some time."

Pastor Hawkins smiled and slowly nodded his head. "We don't need to rush things," he said softly.

After a few minutes of small talk with the pastor, he said he needed to be going and would be in touch in a day or two regarding the funeral.

As soon as he was gone, Mom again brought up the restaurant. Holly could tell her mom was much stronger today and ready to tackle issues such as planning the funeral and overseeing the diner. She decided it was time to ask her mom about Andrew.

"Hank, can you get some coffee for us? I need to talk to Mom about the restaurant."

"More coffee? Okay, sure," Hank said, sounding a bit annoyed that Holly was obviously trying to get rid of him.

Hank ambled out of the room in search of some coffee, leaving Holly to ask her mom about Andrew without her brother hanging around.

"Is everything at the restaurant okay?" Mom said with a bit of concern in her voice.

"Oh, sure. Gary and Eileen have everything under control," Holly said quickly.

"Is something wrong?"

"Mom, Tamron told me that Andrew Preston didn't get married. Then I ran into him at the restaurant, and he told me he comes in several times a week. Why didn't anyone tell me that he and Penelope broke off their engagement? And that he's basically a regular at the family restaurant?"

Mom took a deep breath and looked away. "I suppose we should have, but your dad and I remembered what you went through when things ended with Andrew. Besides, you were seeing someone, that personal trainer, I think, and we didn't want to upset you."

"I went out with that guy for a month, and nothing came of it. Were you afraid I'd run back to Sandalwood to get back with Andrew? You do remember, I'm the one who left town after we broke up."

"It's not that. It's just that, well, we didn't want to complicate your life or cause you any pain."

Holly sighed. She wasn't sure why not knowing about Andrew's broken engagement bothered her so much. But for some reason, it did.

"You're right," Holly said. "I'm sorry I got so upset about it, and I know this isn't the best time to bring it up. I guess it was just a shock to hear out of the blue that he wasn't married."

"It's okay to bring it up. I'm actually thankful to have almost anything occupy my thoughts besides the death of your dad." Mom shifted her weight in the bed, and a pained expression was etched on her face.

Holly felt guilty for being so self-absorbed. "Are you okay? Should I get the nurse?"

"No, I'm fine. It's going to take some time for me to recover. I'm not a young woman anymore." Sadness replaced the pain that was on her face, and Holly knew she was thinking about Dad again.

Now that the fog of the drugs had worn off, the reality of losing her husband of over thirty years was sinking in. "But you seemed more than ready to discuss the funeral a few minutes ago?" Holly said.

"I know. I'm trying to move ahead and do what needs to be done. Your dad would want that."

"I think you should try to get some sleep. I'm going to find Hank and head home. We'll be back sometime tomorrow." Holly leaned down and kissed her mother before heading out to find Hank still wandering the halls looking for coffee.

***

Back at home, Holly opened her laptop and sat down at the kitchen table. She messaged Lora to let her know what was happening. She quickly crafted a message, telling her boss that she would likely want to take a short leave of absence, a few weeks, maybe a little longer. Holly sent the email and then immediately wondered if she had done the right thing.

She thought maybe she could work completely remotely for a month or so. After all, most of her job consisted of doing research and drafting documents. She could do almost all of her job remotely if she had to.

While she was still considering sending Lora another email and revising her work plans while in Sandalwood, she thought she heard Hank talking right outside the house.

He was on his phone. She knew she shouldn't have listened, but it wasn't like she had planned to eavesdrop on his conversation. He was on the porch and must not have realized she was working in the kitchen.

"I'll pay you back as soon as I can," he said in a voice she rarely heard. It was a voice laced with fear. The happy-go-lucky Hank that everyone knew and loved had suddenly disappeared when he thought no one else was around.

"I'm out of town right now... Never mind where I am," Hank said. This time, he sounded angry.

Dozens of thoughts swirled through Holly's mind. Did Hank owe money to a bookie? Maybe a loan shark. Should she confront him and offer to help him pay off the debt?

As he continued to argue with whoever was on the other end, Holly quietly closed her computer and tiptoed out of the kitchen. She didn't want her brother to come in and realize she'd heard his conversation.

When she heard Hank start his van and drive away, she walked out to the front porch. She sat down on the swing and began gently gliding. Her father's death, her mother in the hospital, and Hank with a gambling problem. It was all too much to take. She wasn't sure why, but thinking of Andrew was the only thing that seemed to soothe her nerves.

She realized that all the pain and awkwardness of their breakup didn't seem so bad anymore. They'd basically been kids when that happened. She was glad they were past that now and could enjoy one another's company like adults.

Chapter Six

J oseph Bennett was a beloved and respected man, and the out-
pouring of love and support overwhelmed Holly. It was one of
the things that Holly missed about living in a close-knit community
in the Midwest. Even though Sandalwood was a small town, with a
population of maybe five thousand, Holly figured that at least half the
town had made their way through the funeral home the day before
during the calling hours.

Today, only a few hundred family and friends would attend the
funeral. Holly sat stoically on one side of her mom, who was in a
wheelchair. Hank sat on the other side.

Mom had been released from the hospital the previous afternoon
for the calling. A few days earlier than her doctor had wanted, but
she had insisted she would be there for her husband's funeral. She
was, however, temporarily confined to a wheelchair and told not to
do much walking until the physical therapist gave her the green light.

Pastor Hawkins delivered a beautiful sermon about how Holly's
dad was a man of great faith, and because of Christ's Resurrection,

he would spend eternity in heaven. Holly also missed her small-town church and her conservative, yet kindly, pastor. He delivered biblical truth with conviction, yet was never judgmental.

Holly didn't even notice until the end of the funeral who had slipped in after the service started and was sitting at the back of the church. Andrew Preston and his mother, Lisa, were in the last row.

Now was not the time Holly wanted to have Andrew on her mind. But here he was, looking incredible. He was dressed in a crisp black suit and wearing a cream-colored tie. His wavy dark hair was styled to perfection, and he immediately smiled when she looked in his direction. Holly couldn't help it; she instinctively smiled back.

As soon as she turned back around, she pushed all those unnerving, confusing thoughts of Andrew Preston out of her mind and focused on making sure the rest of the day went as planned.

"Hank, I've got to check with Carol Miller to make sure the lunch will be ready according to schedule," Holly whispered into her brother's ear as everyone began to stand after the funeral service, and soft conversation filled the sanctuary. "See if you can find one of the women in her ladies' group to help Mom to the restroom."

"Don't worry, I'll make sure Mom is taken care of," Hank said, giving his sister a boyish wink.

Holly wasn't sure what to think of her brother anymore. A few days ago, she heard him on the phone, angrily talking about the money he owed some mystery person. Today, he was playing the part of the dutiful son and brother. Hank was a chameleon, but today he was on his best behavior.

Holly had a feeling he was patronizing her, being as nice and helpful as possible so she wouldn't prod him regarding his personal issues. What Hank didn't realize was that Holly was only letting him off the hook temporarily. Right now, she had to focus on making sure Dad's funeral ran smoothly.

There would be a brief service before the burial at the cemetery, and then everyone would return to the church for a late lunch. Thankfully, the restaurant was closed today in honor of her dad. One less thing to worry about.

After talking with Carol Miller, who had been in charge of the Meals Committee for several years, Holly headed up the back stairs toward the sanctuary. She had to make sure Hank was still attending to Mom. She rounded the corner and hurried into the back of the church, nearly running into Andrew.

This was only the second time she had seen Andrew up close and personal since coming back to town. Yet, Holly sensed that they had already reconnected in a way she couldn't quite understand.

As he approached her, she no longer felt nervous or overwhelmed as she had when first seeing him again in the diner.

"Holly," he said softly as he opened his arms for a hug.

She had hugged dozens of people during the last few days, and now, falling into his arms felt as natural as breathing.

She sensed, however, that several people in the church were staring at her and Andrew. At that moment, she didn't care what anyone else in the world thought, and she lingered in his arms.

"Your dad was a wonderful man, and now he's at peace forever," Andrew said, whispering in her ear as he continued to hold her in his arms.

"Thank you," Holly said, slowly pulling back, even though she didn't want to. "Are you coming to the lunch?"

"Mom and I are planning on being there."

"Good. We want everyone who really knew and loved Dad to be with us."

Holly looked over Andrew's shoulder and suddenly saw Lisa standing a few feet behind him. She'd been so preoccupied with Andrew that she hadn't noticed his mom standing close by until now.

Lisa Preston had worked on some of the same committees and ladies' groups at church that Holly's mom had been on, and it was expected that the Preston family would be at the lunch. Holly wondered if it had been awkward through the years for the two of them to work together after she and Andrew had parted ways. If it ever had, her mom had never mentioned it.

After the impromptu hug with Andrew that half the church had seemed to be watching, Andrew excused himself to talk with a friend. That left Holly standing face-to-face with his mother, Lisa.

"You're looking well, Holly," Lisa said firmly. The tone in her voice was polite, but not overly friendly.

"Thanks, so are you," Holly said softly. Holly decided to break through the awkwardness and take the high road. "I want to thank you for being such a good friend to Mom all these years."

Lisa finally smiled. "Your mom and dad have been wonderful friends," she said, fighting back the tears.

"Thank you so much," Holly said.

They both instinctively leaned toward one another for a much-needed hug. In that moment, years of awkwardness due to the breakup between Holly and Andrew melted away. Unfortunately, it took Joseph Bennett's death to bring about this reconciliation.

Holly and Lisa chatted for a few more minutes before Holly excused herself to look for her mom. She finally felt at peace with both Andrew and his mom. But were the feelings she was experiencing regarding Andrew and his mom more than just being able to let go of the past?

After the brief ceremony at the cemetery, everyone was back at the church for lunch. Holly stood at the front doors of the church, staring out into the parking lot and greeting mourners as they headed back inside.

When there was a lull in the crowd, Holly stood by the door and let the cool autumn breeze gush over her face. For a few sweet seconds, her mind was empty, and she felt relaxed. Suddenly, she felt a hand on her shoulder, and the first thought that came to her mind was Andrew.

She glanced over her shoulder and was instantly disappointed that it was Tamron and not Andrew. Even though no one but God knew what she was thinking, Holly felt awkward and exposed for hoping the gentle touch belonged to Andrew.

"Do you need anything?" Tamron asked as soon as Holly spun around.

"Yeah, about fourteen hours of sleep," Holly said, rolling her eyes.

"Yeah, you and me both. There's been a flu bug going around. The kids are both sick and had to stay home with my mom. That's why she couldn't make it."

"I hope they're feeling better," Holly said. "I've got to find where Mom and Hank are. We need to get the lunch started."

***

That evening, Holly sat at the kitchen table and logged onto her computer. Even though she was dead tired, she didn't think sleep would come easily at this point. The funeral was over, her dad was buried, and she had so many jumbled, mixed-up feelings regarding Andrew that she needed to take the time to wind down slowly.

Mom had already gone to bed early, and Hank was in the living room watching television. When he ambled into the kitchen for a snack, she felt the urge to finally confront him about the conversation she'd heard a few days earlier.

"Hank, I have something to ask you," she said.

"Yeah, what is it?" he said, not bothering to pull his head out of the fridge as he rummaged through containers searching for food.

"I know you owe someone money. A few days ago, I heard you on the phone while I was working in the kitchen," Holly said, hoping Hank wouldn't be angry she'd overheard his conversation.

Hank stepped back from the refrigerator with handfuls of containers and a carton of milk shoved under his arm. He had a confused look on his face, and Holly hoped that he wouldn't try to play dumb. He seemed to have a natural knack for that whenever it suited him.

"You were on the porch talking. I was in the kitchen working on my computer," Holly said, trying to make herself crystal clear. "I guess you didn't know I was in here, but I heard at least part of the conversation."

"Oh," Hank said, looking away from Holly.

He set the containers and milk on the counter and started opening and arranging his late-night feast.

"Just tell me what's going on. Do you owe money to a loan shark? I don't want you to get hurt."

Hank adamantly shook his head. "No, it's nothing like that."

"Then tell me," Holly said, more forcefully this time. "I know we don't see each other that much, but we are family."

He let out a long, exaggerated sigh. "I was living with a girl for several months. I was supposed to help pay rent and utilities. I kind of got behind, and I owe her some money. That's all."

"Why would you not want to tell me that?"

"I know how you and Mom feel about people living together before being married. Anyway, it's my problem, and I'll take care of it."

Hank filled a plate full of food, grabbed the carton of milk again, and headed into the living room. Holly sat at the kitchen table, more confused than before. All of a sudden, Hank had a girlfriend he'd been living with for several months? She wasn't sure if this was a completely true story. What she did know was that her brother was in trouble.

Holly was about to go back into the living room to confront Hank and demand some answers when her phone started ringing. She glanced at it and saw it was Tamron.

"Hello," she said, sounding more irritated than she had intended.

"I'm sorry to call now. I know it's late, and you've obviously had a long day."

"Not a problem. What's up?" Holly said, trying to sound more upbeat this time.

"I just want to let you know I'm texting the schedule for volunteers from the church. They'll be coming starting tomorrow, and I've got several scheduled for the next few weeks."

Holly had completely forgotten about how the Ladies Hospitality Committee always provided volunteers whenever someone from the church was sick or hurt. Volunteers would come over in two-hour shifts to help with cooking, housework, running errands, and even with Mom's physical therapy exercises.

"It slipped my mind, but thanks for reminding me."

"Sure. You get a good night's sleep. Bye."

Holly said goodbye, closed her computer, and headed for bed.

Chapter Seven

The following day was Saturday, and Holly woke to a beautiful October sun filtering through the blinds in her bedroom. The funeral was over, and her father was now buried at the Blue Hill Cemetery at the south edge of town. Even though she would miss her dad deeply for the rest of her life, Holly was relieved that the formalities surrounding his death were complete, and she could now take some time to grieve privately on her own.

She stretched her arms, put on her robe, and crawled out of bed. The house and the surrounding neighborhood were incredibly quiet, unlike her apartment and neighborhood in Chicago. She'd barely been gone a week, yet it now seemed as if she'd been away for ages.

Holly went downstairs to get breakfast ready for the three of them. Tamron was on the church schedule to come help out around ten that morning. Even though she'd forgotten about it until last night, she was so thankful the ladies at church had put together a schedule for people to come help out for the next few weeks.

As soon as Tamron arrived, she began cleaning the house while Holly made sure Mom got her breakfast, did a few exercises, and was able to spend some time outside before going back to bed. It was a crisp but lovely autumn morning, and Holly knew it would do her mom good to sit outside in the sunshine while the leaves effortlessly floated to the ground.

Two hours later, Mom was back in bed, and Tamron was folding the last load of laundry and setting the basket on the kitchen table.

Holly smiled. "You're such a good friend. Thanks for helping out."

"Sure. Mom's spending time with the kids today, and I figured I could help out a little bit."

"I should be able to take care of everything myself, but Mom wants me to spend time at the restaurant. I've also got to study for my bar exam. It's scheduled for January."

"And you're still working?" Tamron said, making a face regarding how exhausting all that sounded.

"Actually, my boss just approved my request for a 30-day leave of absence."

"That's a good idea," Tamron said. "What about Hank? Is he helping around here at all?"

Holly sighed. "He did rake some leaves the other day."

Tamron rolled her eyes.

"I know he's still trying to figure out what to do with his life, so I should show him some grace. He left this morning to visit an old friend in town," Holly said.

Tamron shook her head. She'd never been a fan of Hank. "Considering everything that's going on, you're being very generous. But I can tell by the look on your face that there's more going on with Hank than you're telling me."

"There's always something going on with Hank," she said casually. Holly decided it was time to change the subject. "I wonder who's signed up next to come help out. I need to get to the restaurant by noon, and someone needs to help Mom with her afternoon exercises."

Tamron pulled out her phone and opened the church app. "Let's see," Tamron said slowly. "I was signed up this morning. I think it's Virginia Kepler. Uh, no, that's tomorrow. It looks like Lisa Preston is signed up for this afternoon."

Holly felt a lump form in her throat. She and Lisa had made their peace yesterday at the funeral. But Holly had never really spent any time with her since she and Andrew had broken up. Spending time with Lisa would bring back more feelings regarding Andrew that she wasn't sure she wanted to deal with right now.

"I can tell by the look on your face you're not wild about seeing Lisa Preston again," Tamron said.

"Even though our breakup was mutual, it was awkward whenever I was around Andrew's mom after that."

Tamron sighed. "I think it's pretty much like that with almost anyone's parents after a breakup. But it looked like you two were getting along well yesterday."

"Yeah, we did." Holly didn't want to tell Tamron that she was struggling with her feelings for Andrew. "She actually gave me a hug that felt genuine."

Tamron raised an eyebrow and looked as if she were almost ready to start laughing. "Andrew also gave you a big hug yesterday, too."

"Oh, you saw that?" Holly said barely above a whisper.

"Uh, I think the entire church, which is about half the town, saw that."

"Okay, okay," Holly said, obviously irritated. "So, is half the town talking now?"

"Should they be?" Tamron asked.

"Of course not," Holly insisted. "Andrew and I were kids when we broke up. Now we're at a place where we can behave like adults when we're around each other. Dozens of people gave me hugs yesterday. No one is talking about any of those, are they?"

"I suppose not," Tamron said, trying to decide if Holly was protesting a bit too much. "Well, Lisa should be here in less than an hour. I'm about ready to take off. Will you be okay until she shows up?"

"Oh, sure," Holly said. "Mom's resting now. I'll be fine until she gets here."

Holly gave Tamron a quick hug and opened her laptop.

During the next hour, while her mom slept, Holly was able to tie up a lot of loose ends at work. She had some research and a report to finish before she was officially on leave. She sighed, turned off the computer, leaned back, and closed her eyes. Once Lisa arrived, she just might head upstairs and take a much-needed nap and stop by the restaurant later.

"It's still early afternoon, and you're already wiped out?" a voice said from the front porch.

Holly opened her eyes and turned around to see Andrew standing at the screen door.

"Andrew?" she said, practically jumping out of her chair.

He was dressed in a pair of old jeans and a casual button-down shirt, but he looked incredible.

"Can I come in?"

"Uh, sure," she finally said.

"I guess I should have called to let you know Mom is sick and I'm taking her place. It seems every October, the flu bug makes the rounds in Sandalwood. I figured as long as someone showed up, it shouldn't matter."

"Don't you have to work?" Holly asked, forgetting it was Saturday.

"Today is Saturday," he said, giving her a strange look. "October is a pretty slow month for us anyway."

Holly got up from the table and walked toward Andrew. "I guess since Mom can go to the restroom by herself now, it doesn't matter if a man or a woman helps her with her exercises. Lisa was going to run some errands for us, too. Is that okay?"

"I'm at your service for the next two hours."

Holly quickly grabbed a piece of paper and rummaged through the junk drawer to find a pen. She wrote down what Mom needed from the drugstore and the grocery. Then she grabbed the instructions for the exercises the physical therapist had left.

"I'm so glad Mom has people like you and your mom to help her," Holly said, handing everything to Andrew. "When Hank and I are gone, it'll be good to know she has dependable friends like you to help her through everything. That's one more thing I miss about a small town: how everyone looks out for everyone else."

Andrew's fingers lightly touched her hand when he took hold of the papers she was holding. Holly felt a chill run through her body, and she quickly pulled back.

"Are you going back to Chicago soon? It sounds like you might not be sticking around long," he said.

"Oh, I'm not sure. It depends on how quickly Mom recovers. I plan on being here for at least the next few weeks."

Andrew nodded. "Is Caroline in her bedroom or downstairs?" he asked.

"She's in the living room. I'm going to go upstairs and take a nap. I'm beat. If you need anything, just give me a call. I've got my phone with me."

"You get some rest, Holly," he said softly. "I'll take care of everything for the next few hours."

Holly smiled and headed up the back stairs. As soon as she was in her room, she closed the door and crawled under the covers. Seeing Andrew at the restaurant and even the church was one thing. Having him in her home was another.

Even though he was still incredibly attractive and had the same sweet, boyish personality, some things about him had changed during the last eight years. He used to be more skittish, even a bit unreliable. But weren't most eighteen-year-old guys like that? Now, he was mature and dependable. Of course, this just made him all the more desirable to Holly.

She remembered the last night they'd gone out before their breakup. They'd been together in the kitchen, just like they'd been a few minutes earlier. They had argued about their future and how they had wanted different things in life.

Now, here he was again, eight years later, a handsome, successful man. And more than that, a kind man of faith, helping their family after a terrible tragedy. He was too good to be true. There were obviously flaws she couldn't see, just like before. She convinced herself of that as she drifted off to sleep.

***

When Holly woke up about two hours later, she expected Andrew to be gone. She headed downstairs in the same rumpled T-shirt and jeans she'd just slept in and didn't even bother to brush her hair.

She could see her mom sitting on the front porch through the kitchen window and proceeded to open the fridge for a snack.

"Hope you had a good nap," Andrew said, coming in from the porch.

"Oh, yeah," Holly said in a startled voice. She instinctively ran her fingers over her tousled, uncombed hair, thinking how her mascara was almost certainly smudged.

But when Andrew smiled at her the way he did, she couldn't help but feel beautiful.

"I'm getting ready to leave in a minute," Andrew said. "Your mom is doing some reading on the front porch, and Pastor Hawkin's wife is scheduled to stop by later this evening."

"That's good. I need to get dressed and get to the diner. I was planning on getting there earlier, but was so tired."

"That's understandable," Andrew said. "I'm just curious, where's Hank?"

"I'm not sure. He left this morning, and I haven't seen him since. To be honest, I'm kind of worried about him."

"I don't know if I should say this or not," Andrew said, nervously shifting his weight from one foot to the other.

"What is it?" she asked, dreading what she might hear.

"There have been rumors in town that Hank has some issues with gambling." Andrew looked behind him to make sure the kitchen door was completely closed and Holly's mom couldn't hear their conversation. "You know how gossip spreads around here. Hopefully, it's not true, but I just thought you should know."

"Thanks for telling me," Holly said softly. "But I'm afraid it is true."

Chapter Eight

T he next few days were relatively uneventful, and Holly got a lot of studying done for her exam. Hank said he was going to get a few repairs done on the van before heading back to California. Mom offered to pay for the repairs. Holly grumbled to herself that Hank would never become a responsible adult if everyone was always taking care of him, but she didn't say a word to either of them.

But late Wednesday morning, things at the restaurant started to fall apart. As long as Gary and his wife, Eileen, were there, everything ran like clockwork. Gary was a seasoned short-order cook and knew how to turn ham and eggs or a burger and fries into a gourmet meal with only a few ingredients. His wife, Eileen, kept the dining room running smoothly and oversaw all the wait staff.

Steve Graber, a retired teacher, filled in on the few days Gary and Eileen were off. Steve was out of town for the day, visiting his daughter and new grandbaby. So when Gary and Eileen's only car broke down, and they texted Holly to let her know they'd be an hour or so late getting to the diner that day, Holly started to panic.

Holly shut her laptop and called Tamron. Tamron arranged for her mother-in-law to watch the kids and hurried to the diner to help out.

Holly didn't want to tell Mom what was going on. It would only worry her, and she needed as much rest and relaxation as she could get. Besides, she had enough to worry about concerning Hank.

"I'm heading to the restaurant for a while," Holly said, without even going into Mom's room. She didn't want to answer any questions about why she was leaving earlier than she had originally planned.

Within ten minutes, she had her car parked out back and was inside. Tamron arrived a few minutes later.

"So, what's going on? Weren't Gary and Eileen here for the breakfast shift?" Tamron said as she hurried in the back door of the restaurant, meeting Holly by the walk-in refrigerator.

"Yeah, but they had to run an errand out of town, and they left the assistant cook, Mike, in charge between the breakfast and lunch rush," Holly said with a sigh. "Long story short, their car broke down, and it'll be over an hour before they can get back."

"Mike's here. Can't he handle it?" Tamron said softly, making sure Mike wouldn't hear.

"The noon lunch rush is crazy, and no, Mike can't handle it the way Gary can. Besides, Eileen's not here either to make sure the seating goes smoothly and each waitress has the right number of tables."

"Okay, what do you want me to do?"

"I'm going to stay back here and help Mike prep for the lunch rush. I need you to help seat people and make sure none of the girls are overwhelmed. Maybe help them get water and silverware on the tables when customers come in? And make sure they each get an equal number of tables. If they get too many, they'll get overwhelmed. Not enough, and they won't get enough tips."

Tamron did a quick salute and headed to the front of the diner, where the first wave of lunch customers was coming in.

The first twenty minutes were busy, but Mike, Holly, Tamron, and the three waitresses on duty managed to keep everything running smoothly. It wasn't long, however, until things started to go sideways.

When a large group from the hospital came in, Tamron hurried to push two tables together to seat them all and ended up putting together tables from two sections in the diner. Both waitresses started arguing over who would pick up the group since each was responsible for one of the tables. Holly finally decided that they should split the table.

Then several more people came in, and the orders started backing up in the kitchen. After that, it seemed like half of downtown Sandalwood had decided to stop in at the Bennett Diner for lunch.

Holly peeked into the dining room when taking a momentary break from chopping tomatoes and onions for sandwiches. Mom and Dad always insisted that everything had to be made as fresh as possible. Almost every table was full when she pulled an armload of lettuce out of the fridge to make up side salads.

Mike was barely keeping up until kids' orders came back with items that weren't readily on hand. There were also several specials that had substitutions. The Bennetts also liked to cater to anyone who had particular dietary needs.

Bobby Jackson stuck his head in the kitchen and, in a stern but polite tone, asked where his breaded tenderloin and fries were. "I've got to get back to work before too much longer," he said.

"Sorry, Bobby, we'll get it out as soon as we can," Holly said.

"Where's that breaded tenderloin at?" Holly asked Mike.

After Bobby's tenderloin and fries were figured out, each waitress brought in several more orders, an order of fries burned in the deep fryer, and Holly realized she'd just put the wrong dressing on one of the side salads.

"Where's the chicken nugget order?" Tamron asked as she stormed into the kitchen. "That kid's crying out here."

Holly took a quick breath and looked up at the ceiling. She said a quick prayer that God would help them... and keep her from running out the back door and never coming back.

Mike whipped a basket of chicken nuggets out of the deep fryer and practically threw them on a plate. Holly added some fries and pickles and handed the plate to Tamron.

After that, another waitress brought back two more orders.

Holly didn't know whether to laugh or cry. "Just breathe deep," she said, looking at Mike and trying to smile.

"I'm breathing! I'm breathing!" he said while throwing several hamburger patties and a few chicken breasts on the grill.

A few seconds later, Andrew Preston leaned around the kitchen door. "Holly, are you okay?" he said.

"Not really," she said as calmly as possible. "And whatever you ordered probably isn't ready."

"I haven't ordered anything yet. I just came back to see if you guys would like some help."

Holly sighed. "I appreciate the offer, but how much do you know about running a kitchen?"

"A little," Andrew said, walking into the kitchen and grabbing an apron. "I worked at a restaurant one summer when I was in college."

Holly shrugged. "We don't have anything to lose at this point. You help Mike. I'm going to see if I can help Tamron get things straightened out in the front."

Andrew helped Mike get the grill cleaned up and the orders organized. Then he instructed Mike to put a bag of fries in the deep fryer while he fixed the rest of the sandwiches.

Out front, Holly cleaned off dirty tables while Tamron brought water glasses and fresh silverware for several new tables.

As soon as the orders were caught up and everything was relatively under control, Andrew filled the dishwasher and started it.

After helping Tamron at the cash register, Holly downed a glass of ice water. "I think we're going to make it," she said. "I'd better check the kitchen. It's probably a complete mess by now."

Holly headed back to the kitchen. She practically ran into Andrew as he threw open his arms to give her a hug.

"I can't believe we made it through. And it's all thanks to you," she said while wrapping her arms around him.

As she lingered in his arms, she realized how much he had done for her since she'd been back in town. He'd always been a great guy, but all this was almost too good to be true.

He pulled back slightly and gave her that huge smile that always melted her heart.

What happened next seemed to be the most ridiculous yet most natural thing in the whole world. They both leaned in, and before either could even think about what they were doing, Andrew and Holly were kissing.

Holly wanted to stay in his arms forever, but Mike coming out of the freezer with bags full of onion rings and fries caused them both to instantly pull away from each other.

"Think this will be enough to get us through the rest of the lunch shift?" he asked.

Holly looked at Andrew, who had a sheepish grin on his face.

"Looks like enough to me," she said, thankfully realizing Mike hadn't seen them kissing. "But I think you're going to need some more hamburger buns."

"You're right," Mike said and proceeded to rummage through the cabinets next to the stove.

"I'm going to check out front to make sure everything is okay," Holly said.

"But you just came in here," Andrew said.

"It looks like you've got everything under control." She couldn't bring herself to look directly at Andrew and hurried out of the kitchen.

Holly ran into the front of the dining room, as far from the kitchen as she could get. A few customers were still coming in, but most of the tables were starting to empty out.

She couldn't believe what had just happened. She'd kissed Andrew. Or had he kissed her? No, they had both kissed each other.

"Are you okay?" Tamron asked. "Your cheeks are bright red?"

"The kitchen is really hot."

"You need another glass of ice water. I'll get it for you," Tamron said, sounding concerned.

"No, I don't need more water. I just need to sit down."

Holly took a seat at the counter and looked around the restaurant. Was everyone looking at her, or was it just her imagination? She knew how fast gossip spread in a small town like Sandalwood. If even one person saw the kiss or even suspected something was happening between the two of them, it would spread like wildfire.

Andrew came out of the kitchen. "I think Mike can handle it from here," he said. "I'm going to take off."

"But you never even got any lunch," Tamron said.

"There are some doughnuts and coffee in the office," he said. "I'll be fine."

Andrew hurried out the front door without a word to Holly.

Tamron stood there, looking at Andrew as he practically ran out the door, then her gaze came back to Holly.

"What's going on? What happened back there?" she insisted. "Did you two get into an argument or something?"

Holly looked up at Tamron. "No, nothing like that."

"Then what in the world was all that about? And don't tell me nothing."

Holly motioned for Tamron to come closer. "He kissed me," she whispered. "And I think I kissed him back."

Chapter Nine

H olly woke the next morning, finally feeling refreshed. For the first time since coming home, she actually had some time for herself. Everything at the restaurant was under control, ladies from the church were scheduled to spend time with her mom until dinner, and Hank had once again taken off. She decided that it was time to get serious about studying for the bar exam.

She had already downloaded several practice tests and planned to spend the morning studying and going over sample questions. The first hour went smoothly, and Holly felt like she'd already accomplished a lot. Then her mind started to wander. For some reason, she couldn't keep her mind off Andrew and what was obviously happening between them.

Holly knew she was falling in love with him all over again. Maybe she had never stopped loving him. Maybe that was the reason none of the guys she'd gone out with during the last eight years ever turned into real relationships. For the first time, she wondered if the reason

Andrew had called off his engagement to Penelope was because he had realized he'd never stopped loving her as well.

"Stop it," she said to herself out loud. Once she got back to Chicago and into her regular routine, she'd be able to clear her head and figure everything out. She convinced herself that everything that had happened with her dad and being in Sandalwood with Andrew again was clouding her thinking.

When her phone started ringing, she figured it was Tamron or anyone other than who it was. When she looked down and saw that it was Andrew, she gasped for breath. Had she given him her number since returning to Sandalwood, or had someone else?

She thought about not answering. But she found herself unable to not pick up and eagerly say hello.

"Hi, I hope this isn't a bad time," he said.

"No, I'm just sitting at the kitchen table doing some studying," she said, trying to sound casual.

"You're studying for the bar exam, right? How's that going?" he asked, sounding genuinely concerned.

"Pretty good. It's one of those things I don't think you can ever be sure you're ready for."

"Yeah, there are some things in life you can never be fully prepared for."

There was a strange silence between them, and she knew he wasn't talking about studying for an exam any longer.

"Uh, the reason I called is I want to apologize for kissing you. I shouldn't have taken the liberty to just come out and do that," he said.

She took a deep breath and smiled. "You don't have to apologize. It wasn't just you. I think we both kissed each other."

Holly was glad he was bringing this up on the phone and not in person. It was much easier for her to talk with him about it when she didn't have to look him in the eyes. She was glad they had cleared the air and figured that was the end of that. But it wasn't.

"I've taken the day off. I'd like to see you," he said.

Holly sat there for a second, stunned. She wasn't exactly sure what he was asking.

"See me for what?" she asked.

"Unless I totally misread the situation, I think there was more to it than just a kiss in the heat of the moment yesterday. I think I still know you well enough that I didn't misunderstand what was happening. If I'm wrong, just tell me."

Now, even speaking on the phone with Andrew was enough to cause Holly's heart to start racing and her cheeks to flush. "No, you're not wrong," she said softly.

"Gary and Eileen are back at the restaurant, and my mom will be with your mom the entire afternoon. You deserve a few hours to yourself."

"Sure, where do you want to meet?" she said, feeling like a giddy schoolgirl getting asked for a date. She could hear the excitement rising in her own voice.

"The park. Then maybe we could have lunch. As much as I love the diner, we'll go somewhere else."

Holly laughed. "That sounds good. I can be there in an hour."

"Great, I'll meet you by the fountains."

Holly put down the phone, still trying to wrap her head around what was happening. She thought about calling him right back and cancelling. She tried to think of a truthful excuse for why she couldn't see him today. But she couldn't come up with one. Maybe God was trying to tell her something.

She rushed upstairs to shower and dress. An hour later, she was standing in front of the fountains at the local park.

***

It was a gorgeous fall day, and the water in the fountain was glistening in the late morning sun. Holly was worried that she might appear too eager arriving before he had.

She quickly looked around and saw him standing by a cluster of trees overlooking the Samson River. When he saw her, he broke into a wide smile and hurried back to the fountain.

"Sorry, I couldn't resist coming down to the river."

"That's okay," she said. "I know how much you always loved walking on the trails."

Andrew almost reached out and took hold of Holly's hand, but then hesitated and pulled back. She pretended that she didn't notice. Of course, she ached to hold his hand. But she needed to know exactly where this relationship, if it was even a relationship, was heading.

He led the way to the path along the river, with Holly following closely behind. For several minutes, they enjoyed casual small talk and took in the beauty of this incredible day along the Samson River in southern Ohio.

Suddenly, Andrew stopped and gazed out over the water. Holly stood next to him, so close that her shoulder was touching his.

"The day I first saw you at the restaurant, I knew I still felt the same way about you as I did all those years earlier," he said without taking his eyes off the water.

Holly looked away from Andrew and out at the river flowing only a few feet away so peacefully. "I have to admit. I felt the same way, too," she said, turning toward him.

He turned around, this time reaching for her hand without hesitating, and she eagerly embraced the warmth of his touch.

He suddenly had a pensive look on his face, as if he were deep in thought.

"What are you thinking?" she asked, leaning her head on his shoulder.

"I was thinking about why we broke up that summer after graduation."

Suddenly, her muscles tightened up, and her relaxed state floated away like the crackling water down the river. Holly didn't want to talk about anything serious, not now anyway. Why couldn't they just enjoy the moment without rehashing the past?

"You're not saying anything," he said softly. "I guess I shouldn't have brought that up."

"I was just enjoying the moment. I don't know if I'm ready to deal with anything too difficult right now."

Andrew suddenly felt guilty. Holly had just lost her dad, and here he was, suddenly back in her life. "I'm sorry. I know you've gone through a lot lately. It's just that I think we should be up front about what's happening between us, and dealing with the past seems like a good place to start."

Holly knew he was right. They couldn't just amble into some undefined relationship.

"You're right," she finally said. "What about the past should we deal with?"

"Why we broke up, and why after you started college, you hardly ever came back."

"I think part of it was because we were just so young and immature at the time," Holly said, thinking back to the summer of her eighteenth year. "We seemed to argue about so many little things that didn't even matter. As far as not coming back much, I don't know; I figured if I came home a lot, I was bound to run into you living in a small town. I figured if I stayed away, it would be easier to move on with my life."

He gently held her face in his hands. "We're not so young and immature anymore. But one of the big reasons we broke up is still an issue."

"Yeah," Holly said softly.

"We had different goals at the time," he said.

Holly nodded, remembering the last argument they had. The one that hadn't been about little things and had ultimately led to their breakup. "You wanted to stay close to home and go to a community college, while I wanted to go away for school and live in a big city."

"Yeah," Andrew said, thinking back to the same things.

"But Chicago is over five hours away from Sandalwood," Holly said, hoping for a second that Andrew would maybe someday look for an accounting job in the Windy City.

"People have long-distance relationships all the time," he said as if it were no big deal. "It's obvious neither one of us has been able to make a relationship work since we've been apart. I think we owe it to ourselves to try again now that we're older and wiser."

Holly pulled back and looked deep into his eyes. "Maybe I haven't, but you've been engaged! How can you not call that serious?"

Andrew sighed and dropped his head. He then looked up again and out past the river as if he were searching for the right words. "I cared about Penelope. I really did. But I only asked her to marry me because I was lonely and ready to settle down. We both knew it wasn't right not long afterward. That's why we both called it off."

Andrew gently pulled Holly into his arms. "The only woman I ever really loved is you. The moment I saw you in the diner again, I knew you'd be the only woman I ever would love."

With tears in her eyes, Holly leaned in to kiss Andrew. This kiss was different from when they were teenagers and even from the quick, unexpected kiss they'd shared in the kitchen at the diner.

Holly took a deep breath as soon as he pulled away. "So, where do we go from here?" she asked.

"It doesn't really matter to me, as long as we're together," he said.

"Does that mean we're officially together?"

"Is it what you want?" he asked.

She nodded. "What about you?"

He again pulled her into his arms, more closely than before. This answered her question.

Chapter Ten

A s Holly drove back home after spending the day with Andrew, she couldn't remember being this happy in a very long time. She couldn't stop singing along with every song that came on the radio, whether she liked it or not.

Everything seemed to make sense now. Why she was never able to make a relationship work with anyone else and why, whether she had ever admitted it to herself or not, her thoughts would always wander back to Andrew.

She turned the car into the drive and headed toward the house. Holly looked up to the sky and breathed in the crisp country air in Sandalwood, Ohio. She jumped out of the car and ran up the front steps and into the kitchen. She didn't stop at the kitchen table to log into her computer to check her emails. That would have to wait. She had to tell her mom the good news.

"Mom? Where are you?"

"I'm on the back porch," she heard her mom yell from two rooms over.

The strength in her mom's voice told Holly that she was getting better. Everything in their lives was falling into place. After enduring the heartache of losing her dad, the blessings that followed were a sweet reminder that God was constantly caring for each one of them.

"There you are," Holly said, nearly out of breath.

"What in the world is going on? Is everything okay? You were practically running."

"Everything is more than okay. In fact, it's wonderful."

"Really," her mom said, raising an eyebrow. "Where have you been all afternoon that's been so wonderful?"

"I went to the park and then to lunch and then down to the covered bridge... with Andrew."

Holly's mom was surprised, but only for a second.

"So, are you and Andrew a couple again, after all these years?"

Holly nodded and then broke out into a wide grin.

"I'm not surprised, but I am concerned."

"Why?" Holly asked, the look of unfettered joy leaving her face. "I thought you'd be happy for me. You're always asking if I'm seeing someone."

"I am happy for you," Mom insisted. "And Andrew is a great guy. It's just that it didn't work out before, and I hope whatever tripped the two of you up before won't happen again."

Holly sat down next to her mom. "We're several years older now. We're both adults, not teenagers. That's mostly what broke us up the first time."

Mom smiled. It was obvious Holly was so happy, and she hated to burst her bubble, but she had to bring her a little closer to reality. "Do you hear yourself?" Mom asked. "That's *mostly* what broke us up. What about the rest of it? Are you moving back to Sandalwood?"

"Uh, no. I have no plans right now to do that."

"Is Andrew moving to Chicago?" Mom said.

"I don't think so," Holly said softly.

Mom tilted her head and looked straight at Holly. "I don't care how much older and more mature you are now. Long-distance relationships are very difficult to maintain. Wasn't that one of the reasons it didn't work out the first time around? He wanted to stay here and build a life in Sandalwood, and you wanted a life in the big city?"

"I'm not saying it will be easy." Holly stood up and started pacing on the porch. "I thought you'd be happy for me."

"I am. I just don't want you to be disappointed again." Mom shifted her weight in the chair and motioned for Holly to come sit down next to her.

"What?" Holly said once she was sitting. She felt like a small child again, about to be lectured by her mother.

"Losing your dad was a shock to all of us. It's going to take a while to adjust to the fact that he's no longer with us." Mom took hold of Holly's hand. "What I'm saying is that we're all at loose ends emotionally right now."

"You think because of Dad's sudden death, I'm reaching out to Andrew?"

"I'm just saying it's something you should think about."

"I realize now that I've had feelings for Andrew that never went away. And he feels the same way. These feelings were always there. That has nothing to do with Dad's death."

"Even if that's true, you're still living in two different states."

"We'll figure out a way to work it out," Holly smiled and realized it was time to change the subject. "I'm sorry I left you here all day. How have you been?"

"I've been just fine. Lisa Preston was here earlier, and Dorothy Schepp left just before you got here. She worked with me while I did my exercises and then helped me get into the bath. I think I'm ready to be on my own. I can get along fine with the walker and don't really even need that."

"I'm glad you're improving, but let's not rush anything." Holly knew she was telling her mom the same thing about her recovery as she'd told her about her relationship with Andrew.

"Is Hank back yet?" Holly asked, realizing every subject being brought up was a potential minefield.

"No, and I'm getting a little worried."

"I'll see if I can get hold of him," Holly said. She stood up and pushed the walker Mom was now using next to her chair. "Don't stay out too long. The sun will be down soon, and it'll be getting cold."

Holly returned to the kitchen and pulled her phone out of her purse. As wonderful as her day with Andrew had been, reality was now crashing in around her. Mom had made some very valid points regarding her newfound relationship with Andrew. And now she had to worry about her brother.

She pulled up his number on her phone, and surprisingly, he answered after the second ring.

"Where in the world have you been all day?" she asked.

"Hello to you too," he said in a cheerful voice.

Holly could hear loud music and people talking in the background. She could also hear what sounded like a casino. The cha-chings clicking, the electronic whirring, and the distinct sound of a slot machine.

"Hank, where in the world are you?"

"I'm in Columbus, visiting some old friends."

"Hank, stop lying to me! You're in a casino. You're not visiting old friends."

"The roulette wheel is like an old friend. And she's been good to me today. I'll be home in a couple of hours."

***

After fixing dinner, cleaning up the kitchen, and helping Mom to bed, Holly waited for Hank to come home. Her brother was the one loose end in her life that she needed to deal with. She was surprised when he came back earlier than anticipated.

Hank was whistling and practically dancing when he waltzed into the kitchen.

"You've been gambling," Holly said somberly. "And from the looks of things, you've won a little."

"I've actually won a lot," Hank said, unable to stop grinning.

"And you think that will solve all your problems?"

"My financial problems. I made enough to pay off my debt with enough left over to either totally redo the van or invest in a decent car so I can get back to California."

"I'm surprised that van made it to Columbus and back. I'm assuming that's where you were?"

Hank nodded and laughed. "Like there are casinos in Sandalwood."

Holly wanted to know what he was going to do with that junky van if he bought a new car, who the van belonged to, and if they cared if he left it in Ohio when he got a new vehicle, but she didn't have the energy to ask.

"Hank, it will only solve your financial problems temporarily, and it won't even touch the deeper issues in your life you're avoiding."

Hank sighed. "Are you going to preach to me again about church and God?"

"No, you should know enough by now about church and God to make better decisions regarding your life."

Instead of getting angry, Hank only stared out the window, momentarily gazing at the rising moon. He smiled and then headed upstairs.

Holly decided to get some studying in before calling it a night herself. A few hours later, she closed her laptop and decided to take a hot bath. She did, however, want to talk to Andrew before going to bed that night. She picked up her phone and saw that she had a missed call and a text from him.

She'd forgotten how early he went to bed, how early most people went to bed in a small town.

She read the text several times before putting her phone down.

Hope you have a good night. Sweet dreams, my beautiful girl.

***

The next morning, Holly was up and out of bed by seven. She'd never been so excited to start her day as she was now. The pain of losing her dad to an untimely death would probably always be with her. But now, she had the love of Andrew back in her life.

After making sure Mom was cared for before the first volunteer showed up, Holly spent the rest of the morning at Tamron's house, helping out with the kids. She couldn't wait to tell her every detail about Andrew.

"You don't have to help change diapers and clean up the baby's room," Tamron said.

"You've done so much since Dad passed. Everything you did with the funeral, helping with Mom, and with the restaurant. This is the least I could do."

"Your parents have been like a second family to me. But changing diapers, that's not your style."

"Maybe I should get some practice in. Who knows when it may come in handy?" Holly said with a mischievous grin.

"Are you thinking about having a baby? I didn't even know you were seeing someone."

"I wasn't seeing anyone until, oh, yesterday afternoon."

It only took Tamron a second to figure out who Holly was referring to. "You and Andrew are back together? After one kiss?"

"What's been happening between us has been a lot deeper emotionally than one kiss," Holly said excitedly.

"I'm really happy for you," Tamron said. "I should have seen this coming a mile away."

"I don't know why you should have seen it coming," Holly said with a laugh. "I sure didn't."

Chapter Eleven

T he next week was the most wonderful of Holly's life. Her schedule consisted of helping in the restaurant each day, spending time with Mom, and then seeing Andrew every evening when he got off work. She also managed to squeeze in a few hours of studying for the bar exam, making her daily life full and deliriously happy.

She was grateful that Lora had approved her brief leave of absence. Once she hopefully passed the bar, she would have to decide if she wanted to continue working at Sherman and Oaks, practicing finance law, or branch off into another legal area.

Mom was getting better every day, and even though Hank had not promised to get help for his gambling, he had finally agreed to go to church with them. Holly hoped that in the long run it would lead him to the right path in life.

It was Friday night, and Andrew had invited her over for a home-cooked meal. He was going to cook Italian for both of them.

Holly chuckled as she stood in front of the mirror selecting earrings that went with her outfit.

Years ago, they had both joked that he didn't know how to boil water, and she wondered what kind of Italian dinner she was getting herself into. She suddenly realized she didn't care, as long as they were together.

Mom began to smile when she saw Holly waltzing down the stairs, dressed in a skirt and a fancy sweater.

"Off to Andrew's again?" Mom said as she pushed her walker between the kitchen table and the sink.

Holly knew her mom well enough to know her tone of voice, and what she said was not so much a question as a statement.

"Are you upset about me seeing Andrew?" Holly asked.

"Of course not. It just seems that everything is happening so fast."

"We're not in high school or even college anymore," Holly said firmly. "We're older, more settled, and know what we want."

"I know," Mom said, softening her tone. "But you've only been home a few weeks. You've both been living separate lives for years. That's a very short time to pick up where you left off, no matter how old you are."

Hank barrelled down the stairs like he was in high school again. He grabbed a mug and poured coffee. Holly was irritated that he never made any coffee but always seemed to drink his share.

"Did you hear what I said?" Mom asked.

"Yes, and in some ways I agree with you," Holly said, surprising her mom. "The difference is, we're not picking up where we left off. We're starting brand new, from where we're both at now."

"You both have lived quite a bit of life since your time together," Mom said, giving Holly a look that took only a few seconds to figure out.

"Are you talking about Penelope? They broke off their engagement nearly a year ago."

"I know, but they were together for over a year before that. I'm not saying he wants to get back with her. I'm just saying, sometimes, it takes longer than you think to get over things like that."

"Andrew has assured me that everything is over between them," Holly said confidently.

Mom gave Holly her worried look, then turned her attention to Hank. "How is it going with the van? Do you have it running yet?"

"I'm going to sell the van and give the money to my friend in Los Angeles. I'm off to Mike's used car lot before they close tonight to look for another car for myself."

Well, at least that explained what Hank was going to do with the van, but now Holly wondered if he'd actually tell Mom where he got the money for a new car.

"A new car?" Mom said, shaking her head in disbelief. "Where in the world did you get the money to buy a new car?"

"It's not a new car. It's used. And don't worry, Mom. It's all figured out. And no, I didn't do anything illegal to get it."

"Did you get the money for the car gambling?" Mom asked, the disappointment obvious in her voice.

Hank kissed Mom on the cheek and rushed out the front door.

Mom sighed and then looked in Holly's direction. "You have a good time this evening," she said weakly.

"Thanks, Mom. Are you going to be okay alone while I'm gone?"

"I'm going to fix supper and then probably go to bed early. I'm going to the restaurant with you tomorrow."

Holly looked surprised. She hadn't even thought that Mom might start going in yet. She knew, however, that she was improving so much that she was starting to get bored just mulling around the house most days.

"Are you sure you're up for it?" Holly said.

Mom nodded. "It's time. I need to get back into a regular routine again."

Holly nodded, kissed her mom on the cheek, and headed out the door to Andrew's.

***

A beautiful golden moon was rising in the sky as Holly got out of her car and headed toward Andrew's front door. It was what farmers often called a harvest moon.

It was a warm evening for early November, and Andrew had left the front door slightly open. It was one more thing Holly missed about living in a small town. Everyone felt safe leaving doors and windows open, and hearing the sounds of nature added to the ambience of a family gathering or a small romantic dinner.

The smell wafting through the screen door and out onto the porch was incredible. "Whatever you're cooking smells amazing," Holly said as she walked into the living room.

Andrew came out of the kitchen and gave her a hug. "I'm fixing pasta primavera," he said with a smile. "I've set up the living room like that Italian restaurant we went to for our senior prom."

She looked toward the front window and saw a card table set up with a checkered tablecloth over the top and a vase full of flowers in the center. Holly thought fondly of the little restaurant near Columbus that Andrew had taken her to before the prom. The aroma that filled his entire house suddenly brought back many fond memories.

She walked into the kitchen and nearly laughed out loud. Everything was a mess. Dirty dishes were in the sink, towels were strewn across the counter, and open jars and little bags of spices were sitting haphazardly everywhere. But when she took the lid off the olive oil and butter sauce, she could tell it was wonderful.

Holly leaned her head down into the steam and took in the amazing aroma. At that moment, Andrew came from behind and wrapped his arms around her waist.

"All that's left is to light the candles, and then we'll be ready to eat," he said softly into her ear.

As he held her in his arms, gently swaying back and forth, Holly felt as if her feet would leave the floor and they would fly into the clouds together. She decided at that moment to tell him what was in her heart, what she was really thinking. She turned around, pulled back slightly, and steadied herself.

"I've been thinking about something," she said softly.

"I've been thinking about a lot of things lately," he said with a wide grin. "You go first."

"I've already taken a short leave of absence from my job so I can stay in Sandalwood until Mom recovers enough to live on her own." Andrew nodded, and Holly stopped to take a breath before continuing.

"I was thinking of maybe taking a longer leave of absence, maybe seeing if I can work remotely indefinitely, or at least for a few months. What do you think?"

"This is what I think." Andrew leaned down and kissed Holly more passionately than she had ever been kissed in her life.

While they were still kissing, someone started knocking on the front door.

"Can you get that?" Andrew said, finally letting go of Holly. "The sauce is almost ready."

Holly was so happy, she was practically waltzing to answer the front door. She swung open the door to find Penelope Gables standing on the front steps.

Holly was speechless. Seeing Penelope was the last thing she had expected that evening. Penelope was even more elaborate than she had remembered. With her blonde puffy hair, dark makeup, and fuzzy pink sweater, she looked like a 1950s pinup girl.

"I need to see Andrew," she said curtly.

It took all of Holly's strength to politely say, "Sure, come in."

She headed to the kitchen to get Andrew.

"Wait until you see the dessert I made," he said with a big smile.

"Andrew, Pen—"

He interrupted her and leaned in for a quick kiss.

Holly pulled back and took hold of his shoulders. "Andrew, Penelope is here. Did you know she was coming over tonight?"

Andrew's face turned pale. "No, I didn't." He put down the dish towel he was holding and headed to the front door.

Holly stood in a place in the living room where she could easily observe both their faces. She carefully watched their expressions as their eyes met. Penelope looked calm, casual, and totally in control of herself. Andrew seemed awkward and nervous.

"Penelope, what are you doing here?" he said.

"Andrew, I need to talk to you," she said in a syrupy voice that sounded totally different than the voice she'd used a minute ago. "Can you step outside?"

Holly expected him to say, *No, whatever you have to say, you can say it in front of Holly*. But he didn't.

Even though they were only outside for a few seconds, Holly felt as if everything changed in those brief moments.

When they came back inside, Holly attempted to remain calm and in control. She didn't want Penelope to know how much this was bothering her.

Andrew stood facing Holly with his back to Penelope. "She just stopped by to pick up a few things," he said somberly.

Holly thought to herself, *Pick up a few things? Why in the world would she need to pick up anything at this point? Hadn't their engagement ended nearly a year ago?*

She stood frozen in place, trying to keep herself together as Penelope walked into the house with a smug grin on her face.

Chapter Twelve

H olly was unable to move as Penelope marched into the house. Penelope was everything Holly wasn't—voluptuous, blonde, and bold as brass.

"Go ahead and get your things," Andrew said when he turned back around to face Penelope.

"Penny's here to pick up a few things," he said again nervously to Holly.

"Penny? Pick up a few things? I thought your engagement ended almost a year ago," Holly said as soon as Penelope walked past them and headed into Andrew's bedroom.

"It did. But she had already started moving her things in with me."

"You two were living together?" Holly said, trying to keep her angry voice to a whisper.

"No, but once we had been engaged, she had started to bring things over."

Penelope went into Andrew's bedroom and started digging through the back of the closet. She came out a few minutes later with a pair of boots and a winter coat.

Holly and Andrew stood in the living room, looking awkwardly at anything but each other, when Penelope came back out.

She had a wide grin on her face. "It's getting colder out. I'm going to need these things in another month or two. Thank you, Andrew. You're a dear," she said before strutting out the front door.

Holly took slow, deep breaths, waiting until Penelope was out of the house and getting into her car before saying anything else. "Why didn't she take them when you broke up?"

"She did take most of it. I guess she forgot a few things."

"And she conveniently remembers it after all this time, when I happen to be here?"

"What are you implying?"

"Maybe you two aren't as broken up as you say you are?"

"What does that mean?"

"Will you let me see your phone if I ask?" Holly said, trying to sound calm and rational while asking something she wasn't sure was even appropriate.

"Why do you want to see my phone? Ask me what you want to know. Either you trust me or you don't," Andrew said firmly.

"I want to see the last time you two have texted or called one another."

"Holly, that's childish. If you don't trust me anymore than that, I'm not sure what kind of relationship we're going to have."

"So, you're not going to let me see it?"

"Holly, either you trust me or you don't. If you want to know something, just ask me."

"Okay, have you and... *Penny* texted or called one another since you broke off the engagement?"

Andrew hesitated and then looked directly at Holly. "A few times, but not since you've been back in town."

Holly's hurt expression was more than Andrew could take, and he immediately started to explain. He said that they had wanted to remain friends and that they occasionally called and texted one another. His words came out quick and jumbled.

Holly wasn't sure if what he was saying simply didn't make any sense or if she was too upset to process it right now. Either way, his explanation just seemed to be little more than rambling nonsense.

She suddenly noticed there was a strange odor coming from the kitchen. "What's that smell?" Holly said.

"The pasta sauce," Andrew cried. "It's burning!"

They both ran into the kitchen to find Andrew's gourmet sauce boiling over and burning on the stove.

"I've lost my appetite, anyway," Holly said.

Andrew turned off the stove, quickly took the pan, and set it in the sink. "We obviously need to talk about this," he said somberly.

"I think this was a mistake. We rushed into this relationship much too fast," Holly said, fighting back the tears.

"Yes, it is fast, but we have a history together. And I know you've been feeling what I've felt."

She took a deep breath and gently pushed him away. "Maybe we can talk when we're calmer. I'm going home. Please, don't try to stop me."

Holly turned and walked out the door. A part of her wanted to get away from him as quickly as she could. Another part, however, wanted him to try to stop her. But he didn't.

***

Holly had spent the last hour driving around Sandalwood, listening to music, and trying to figure out what was going on in her life. When she finally came home, she didn't expect anyone to still be up. But both Hank and Mom were sitting in the living room watching a movie. They were both laughing and talking, and it was obvious Mom was feeling much better.

Holly stopped in the kitchen to compose herself before going into the living room. She didn't want to tell them what happened, not tonight anyway. She needed time to figure it out herself and to try to get a good night's sleep. Besides, they both seemed so happy right now.

She wiped her eyes and checked her reflection in the window. Since only the TV was on in the living room, hopefully it would be dark enough that they wouldn't be able to tell she'd been crying.

"Hey, Mom, I thought you were going to bed early?" she said as cheerfully as possible.

"I was, but Hank talked me into watching this old romantic comedy," Mom said. "You want to watch the rest of it with us? You used to love this movie."

"Thanks, but I'm pretty tired. I'm going to go to bed."

"Holly's living her own romantic movie," Hank teased. "She doesn't need to watch this old stuff."

Holly faked a laugh. "You two have fun. See you in the morning," she said.

"Good night, dear," Mom said, while Hank waved and smiled.

After changing for bed, Holly fell on her knees and cried out to God, asking why everything in her life had gotten so crazy in just a few short weeks. Even though she didn't seem to be getting any answers, she did feel better after pouring her heart out in prayer.

She crawled into bed and fell asleep faster than she thought she would.

Holly woke the next morning, still without answers, but at least with a plan for what her next step would be.

"It's time to go back to Chicago," she whispered to herself as she stared into the mirror at the dark circles under her eyes.

As she continued to stare at the face in the mirror, eight years older but obviously not eight years wiser, she chided herself for getting into a relationship again so quickly with Andrew. She tried to convince herself she'd simply been vulnerable because of Dad's death. Yes, she obviously still had feelings for Andrew, but she wouldn't have jumped into his arms so quickly if she hadn't already been an emotional wreck.

She pulled out her suitcase and started packing.

But before making her final decision, Holly wanted to talk to Tamron. She'd hardly spoken to her since reuniting with Andrew. She left a note for Hank and Mom and took off for Tamron's house.

Even though it was Saturday, her husband was pulling out of the drive for work as Holly pulled in. She waved and pasted on a smile as he drove past. Holly was so tired of putting on an act in front of everyone that she broke down sobbing as soon as she was in Tamron's kitchen.

"Holly, what happened? Is your mom okay?"

Holly nodded and took a breath to calm down.

"Is it Hank? Is he in some kind of trouble?"

"It's me and Andrew. It's not going to work out."

"You and Andrew? I thought things were going so well." Tamron got up, reached for a handful of tissues, and gave them to Holly.

Holly blew her nose and wiped her eyes. "Everything was going well. Until Penelope showed up at his house last night unexpectedly," she said, trying not to sound bitter. "At least he said it was unexpected."

"Penelope showed up? Why was she there?"

"She came to pick up items she'd left at his house when they were engaged," Holly said with a snarky voice.

"You've got to be kidding me. He called off the engagement months ago."

"Since they broke up, have you ever seen them together after that or heard anything about them?" Holly asked.

"Never, on both counts," Tamron insisted. "They've been broken up all this time, and now, all of a sudden, since you're here, she's back in the picture?" Tamron started shaking her head.

"What are you thinking? Do you think it's just Penelope, that she's trying to cause trouble for us?"

"I wouldn't put it past her," Tamron said.

"I should have known better than to allow myself to fall in love with him again so quickly."

"It's just one argument. You guys will get past this."

"If it was just one run-of-the-mill argument, I'd say you were right. But there's more to it than that." Holly was still crying but somehow managed to keep her voice steady.

"Why would you think that?" Tamron reached for the tissue box. She pulled out several more tissues and quickly handed them to Holly. "Listen," Tamron continued, "Penelope has always been known as, how shall we say this? She's known as a man-eater around town, to put it nicely. She's just trying to come between you and Andrew because you're together now, not because there's anything left between the two of them."

Holly wiped her eyes and blew her nose several times. "I thought that too, until I asked Andrew to give me his phone."

"What was on his phone?" Tamron said cautiously.

"I don't know. He wouldn't give it to me, but he admitted they've never completely stopped texting or calling each other during the last year."

Tamron took a moment to process the information. "Maybe they're just trying to stay friends and keep things cordial. I mean, she's dated other people since they broke up. He really hasn't gone out with anyone for almost a year. Not that I know of, anyway."

"That's what he said. It's just that there still seems to be a connection between them."

"What else did he say about it?"

Holly sighed. "He says they're just friends and that he didn't want there to be bad feelings. He says he wants to maintain a friendly relationship because they live in a small town and are bound to run into each other."

Tamron nodded. "That does make sense."

"I guess. The worst thing is, he never told me he was still talking to her, and he wouldn't let me see his phone."

Tamron was pacing the kitchen floor, trying to come up with logical answers. "You guys did get back together pretty fast. Maybe in the craziness of everything going on... well, he..."

"It slipped his mind that he's talking to his ex-fiancée?" Holly interrupted.

"I don't know, maybe?" Tamron was running out of comforting things to say.

Holly stood up and walked to Tamron's kitchen window. She gazed out at the rambling backyard as if the answers were out there somewhere.

"My mom is right, and what you said about getting back together so fast is right," Holly finally said. "I think it's time I go back to Chicago. Mom is almost better now, and Gary and Eileen basically run the restaurant."

"Now you're just making another rash decision," Tamron said.

Holly shook her head. "I need to go back, at least for a little while. To clear my head, I need to get out of Sandalwood."

Chapter Thirteen

The November wind in Chicago was cold and dreary. The weather, however, seemed to fit Holly's mood. She didn't tell anyone she was back, including Lora. She stayed holed up in her apartment, spending her first few days just studying. She only ventured out to pick up food and other necessities.

She called home every morning to check on Mom. Of course, Mom was worried about her, but she actually agreed that getting away, at least for a while, was a good idea. Holly promptly deleted all texts and calls from Andrew.

After several days back in Chicago, she went to her favorite seafood restaurant and indulged in succulent shrimp scampi and crab legs. Bright and early the next morning, Holly took the train as she had always done and headed for the office. She wanted to get there before everyone else did to talk to Lora.

Everything at Sherman and Oaks Law Firm looked the same, but it all felt different. Odd was perhaps the word Holly was looking for. During the last few days, she had tried to immerse herself in her old life, convincing herself that she could step back into the past and everything would be as it was before she had received that awful phone call in the middle of the night.

There were only a few people in the office when she arrived, and one of them was her boss, Lora.

"I knew you'd be here before eight, with your nose to the grindstone," Holly said as she walked into Lora's office.

"Hey, stranger! It's great to see you," Lora said, getting up and giving Holly a hug. "But I thought you were going to be on your leave of absence for a bit longer?"

"About that," Holly said. "Everything wrapped up back in Sandalwood more quickly than I thought it would. If you need me back sooner, I'm ready."

"Of course, we need you. We're super busy right now. But don't feel rushed. After losing your dad so unexpectedly, I don't blame you for needing some extra time off."

Holly forced a smile and tried to keep her emotions concerning both her dad and Andrew under control. "I appreciate that. But I think during the last few days, I realized what I need most right now is to get back to work. I need to get back into my routine again."

"If that's what you need, we're more than glad to have you back."

Holly smiled and glanced around the office. "I think I'll start coming in more and only work remotely a day or two each week."

Lora nodded and walked with Holly as she headed back to her cubicle. There was a light layer of dust over her desk, files, and other items lying sprawled haphazardly. It was all the way she had left it when she had unknowingly worked her last day several weeks earlier.

When Holly left work that day, she tried to maintain the enthusiasm she'd felt earlier that morning. But the weather was windy and dreary, the ground wet and dirty, and the train ride back to her apartment noisy and annoying. Had it always been this way? Or had she never really noticed it before? Maybe she had, and it simply hadn't bothered her.

Once she got off the train, the streets seemed more crowded and the people more unfriendly than she remembered. After spending several weeks in Sandalwood, the contrast between Chicago and a small town was more apparent than ever.

Holly realized that every other time she'd been home since leaving after high school, it had only been for a few days at a time. The weeks she had just spent in Sandalwood had left a profound impact on her. For the first time since leaving home at age eighteen, she wondered if she had made the right choice, whether Andrew was in her life or not.

***

She'd talked to her mom several times since being back to make sure everything was okay. Except for some aches and pains, she was pretty much recovered. She only used the walker a little bit at the end of the day when she was tired. The shock of losing her husband of over thirty years was over, but the daily reminders that he was gone and the pain that accompanied it were there on a regular basis.

Holly was dealing with her own sense of shock and loss. Those few weeks in Sandalwood had caused her serious emotional whiplash. Before going back, she hadn't seen or talked to Andrew in years. In a few short weeks, she'd fallen for him again, they'd gotten back together, and then broken up again just as quickly. And now she was back in Chicago as if everything was back to the way it was before. On top of that, she'd had a strained reunion with her brother, Hank.

Later that day, several of Holly's friends from the office invited her out to dinner that evening. She told herself she was ready to get back in the swing of things and start socializing again, and had told them she'd meet them later at one of their favorite restaurants.

Holly took a deep breath and stared at her computer screen. It was late afternoon, and she didn't have the energy to focus on work any longer. She turned off her computer and got ready to leave for the day. She thought about stopping by the church she attended in Chicago and seeing if the pastor was available.

Holly decided to call first, and when the office manager said he was out for the rest of the day, she headed back to the apartment. She'd take a long, hot shower, get dressed, and then meet her friends for dinner.

The restaurant was only a few blocks away, and the walk in the brisk evening air would do her good. She was just about ready to leave the apartment when she heard her phone ringing. She quickly picked it up and saw the call was from Andrew. He had stopped trying to call for several days, and she thought she'd never hear from him again.

She didn't want to answer, but what if it was about her mom? She reasoned that if it was important, he'd leave a message. She waited and then checked the phone again. There was a message.

Holly, I hope you've had time to think about everything. I certainly have. I should have told you I was still talking with Penelope. But everything happened with us so quickly, and since I hadn't talked to her since you came back to town, I just didn't think about it. I'm sorry. I really love you, and I want you back.

Warm tears filled Holly's eyes. She wanted so badly to believe that everything he'd just said was true. She just didn't know what to believe. Holly thought about texting him back, but had no idea what to say.

She texted her friends, telling them she was exhausted and was skipping their dinner. She changed into her pajamas, crawled under the covers, and went to bed for the night.

Holly woke up at midnight after several hours of restless sleep. She sat at the edge of her bed, staring out over downtown Chicago. How many times before had she sat there and admired the glitzy lights of the city? It suddenly looked completely different. Everything from the sky to the buildings seemed colorless and gray.

She'd attended college in Indianapolis and then moved to Chicago within a month of graduation. For about six months, she'd worked at a small law firm before starting the position of Lora's legal assistant at Sherman and Oaks. She'd gone from one big city to an even bigger one, following her dream.

She loved her job, and her career was going well, but maybe it was time for a change. She'd been at Sherman and Oaks for almost four years. She'd hopefully be passing her bar exam soon. The more Holly thought about it, the more she realized that as much as she liked Lora and the firm she worked for, it was time to move on to something different.

The next morning, when the chapel was open, she walked into the main sanctuary. She took a seat near the front and stared up at the cross. Bending down on her knees, Holly bowed her head and spent the next several minutes praying earnestly.

Dear Lord, I'm not trying to test you; really, I'm not. But I need a sign. Please tell me what the next steps in my life need to be.

She remained on her knees for several minutes, taking in the sweet solitude of the chapel. She didn't really feel that she had an answer to her prayer, but she did feel a sense of peace and calm that had eluded her earlier.

After leaving the chapel, Holly realized how incredibly hungry she was. She stopped at a little diner for some breakfast before going back to her apartment to get some work done.

The couple seated next to her were chatting and laughing and occasionally holding hands. She couldn't help but notice them while she ordered a vegetable omelet and a cup of coffee.

A few minutes after ordering, the server brought Holly a large plate of biscuits and gravy, with extra pickles on the side and a root beer! She looked down at the plate and then back up at the server.

"This isn't my order. I ordered a veggie omelet."

"Oh, that's my order," the man at the next table said with a silly expression on his face.

The lady beside him affectionately rubbed his arm and rolled her eyes. "He always orders everything with extra pickles and a root beer."

She suddenly thought of Andrew and felt a chill run through her body. If this wasn't a sign, she wasn't sure what would be. Holly smiled as the server picked up the plate and glass and delivered them to the other table.

The most beautiful memories she had of her time with Andrew, her family, and friends in Sandalwood all swept through her mind. It wasn't an overwhelming sign with thunder or flashes of lightning. But there was a surety and contentment in her soul that she believed was unmistakable.

She knew she had jumped to a conclusion and had been hasty and emotional regarding Andrew – just as she had been years earlier. And even if it didn't work out with her and Andrew, it didn't matter. It was time to come back to Sandalwood, Ohio, for good.

Chapter Fourteen

H olly took the long way when returning home, driving straight through downtown Sandalwood. It was the middle of November, and holiday decorations were everywhere. A large fake turkey was on the front steps of the courthouse. Pumpkins were lining the sidewalks.

Holly pulled into the driveway at home. A car was there that she didn't recognize. If Mom had company, she probably wouldn't ask a million questions about why she was back again so soon. This would give Holly time to settle in before explaining everything. But company was not what she found when coming into the kitchen.

Hank was sitting at the kitchen table, eating a large ham sandwich with a mountain of potato chips on the side. The first thing she thought was, *good, that brother of mine needs to gain a few pounds.*

As soon as Hank saw his sister, he set the sandwich down, and he widened his eyes. "You're back home. Is everything okay? What's going on?"

"Everything is fine. In fact, it's more than fine," Holly said, setting her purse and jacket on the table.

"Great to see you as always," he said. "Is this going to be a long visit or a short one?"

"I'm coming back to Sandalwood permanently," she said.

"Now, wait. I can't keep up. Are you and Andrew back together again?" he asked.

"No. But I decided I'm coming back to Sandalwood whether we're together or not. Since you just gave me the third degree on my life, what about you?"

Hank smiled. "Just so you know, I'm staying permanently in Sandalwood, too."

"Really?" Holly was genuinely surprised.

"Pastor Hawkins is helping me get into a program for gambling addicts. I'm also looking for a full-time job, maybe in construction. I did work on a construction site a few years ago."

Holly had rarely felt such joy in her life. She ran up to her brother and threw her arms around him. "I am so glad to hear that, Hank."

Hank smiled shyly. "Yeah, well, don't expect perfection."

"I'll never expect perfection. I just want you to make an effort to improve your life. You're clearly doing that now." She hugged him again and then asked where Mom was.

"She's out shopping with friends," Hank said.

"Who picked her up?"

"No one. She's driving again."

"This family is going to be okay," she said, giving her brother another hug.

"So what are you going to do? Look for a law job in Sandalwood? I don't want to rain on your parade, but there are probably not too many of those."

Holly shrugged. "I know. If I can't find something here or in anoth-er nearby small town, I could probably find something in Columbus. Yeah, it's an hour away, but maybe I could commute once or twice a week and work the rest of the time remotely. Right now I'm focusing on studying for the bar. I'm taking it in January. I've got enough saved that I'll be fine for the next few months."

Hank nodded and smiled.

"Help me get my things in from the car," Holly said excitedly.

For the next twenty minutes, Hank helped Holly unload the car and carry everything up to her bedroom. "Is this everything from your apartment in Chicago?" he asked.

"Oh no, I've got a lot more, plus furniture I put in storage. I'll have it sent here when I finally get a place of my own."

"So, you won't be staying at Mom's long?"

"Just until I pass the bar and get a new job," she said enthusiastically. "What about you?"

Hank shrugged. "Not sure, gonna play it by ear. When talking with Pastor Hawkins, he suggested I stay here at least until I'm finished going through my counseling for gambling. He thinks it's good for me to be around a strong source of support. Besides, right now, Mom probably needs me around as much as I need her."

"That sounds like a good plan," Holly said. "Speaking of Mom, when do you expect her back?"

"You know how she and the ladies get when they're talking."

"Yeah, I know," Holly said with a chuckle. "I'm going to take off for a bit. If Mom comes home before I get back, don't tell her I'm here. I want to surprise her."

***

Holly wasn't sure where she was going at first. She pulled out of the drive and just took off. It wasn't long, however, before she realized that she was heading to the park and the river.

She wanted to think about Andrew, to sense his presence, but she definitely wasn't up to seeing him. She knew eventually she'd run into him again, probably on a regular basis. Living in a small town again made that inevitable. But she wanted some time to process everything that had happened, to come to some kind of peace about it all.

Finally, after walking the entire length of the trail, she came to the covered bridge. The beauty that had engulfed the bridge in the height of autumn, even a few weeks ago, was now gone. The leaves had all fallen, the trees were bare, and the sky was gray and dreary.

Holly felt tears forming in her eyes as she walked across the bridge. Even though the bridge was covered, the sides were open, and she could lean over the edge of the bridge and stare into the creek below.

She was still standing along the side, on the walkway, when she heard a car coming by. She turned around quickly and waved. It was Barry Jepsen, an old farmer going by in his truck.

She continued to walk; the crunch of leaves beneath her feet was familiar and soothing. Every few yards, she would stop and gaze over at the trickle of water flowing below. She was almost across the bridge when she stopped again to look over the side. This time, the sound of the crunching leaves didn't stop when she did. There was someone walking behind her.

She was suddenly afraid, and her Chicago instincts kicked into gear. She spun around to see Andrew walking about ten yards behind her.

"I'm sorry. I hope I didn't scare you," he said.

Chapter Fifteen

"How did you know I'd be here?" Holly asked.

"I didn't. I didn't even know you were back in town." Andrew took a deep breath and walked toward her. "But I'm glad you are here. All I'm asking is that you give me a few minutes to explain everything."

She could sense his sincerity, but was so afraid to let him into her heart again after everything that had happened.

He took hold of her hands and looked into her eyes.

"There's been absolutely nothing romantic between Penelope and me since we broke up nearly a year ago. I wanted things to remain friendly, especially since we live in the same small town and are bound to run into one another. So, yes, we texted occasionally. I was wrong to keep it from you. But everything happened so fast between us that I didn't even think to tell you, and when I did, I feared you wouldn't understand... that you would leave."

The wind whipped up, sending a chill down Holly's back and causing her to relish in the warmth of Andrew's hands. "And I did leave," she said, barely above a whisper. "I ran away, just like I did all those years ago after high school."

"But this time you came back a lot sooner. Why did you?" he asked.

"I decided that it's time to come home and start a life here, no matter what happens with us. Not that I don't want something to happen with us, but it has to be different than before, slower perhaps."

Andrew nodded. "I completely agree. I was just so excited when I first saw you in the diner that day. I could sense there was still something between us after all those years. I also knew that you were vulnerable. Your dad had just passed away, and I needed to take things slow. But I didn't. I pushed headfirst into a relationship with you again because I knew I had never stopped loving you."

Holly smiled. "I felt the same way, too. Everything started to make sense in my life after coming back home. I know now that my life is here, and I want you to be part of it."

***

When Holly got back home that evening, she realized she didn't feel the same giddy teenage excitement about Andrew as she had before. Sure, she was both excited and hopeful. But things were different now. They were developing a calmer, more mature love that would hopefully last a lifetime.

What she sensed now more than anything was peace. She knew she'd made the right decision to come back to Sandalwood and start a new life. She also knew she was meant to be with Andrew. But this time they weren't going to rush into a relationship like a couple of hormonal teenagers. It was going to be based on a solid friendship, communication, and a shared faith.

Mom's car was in the driveway, and Holly wondered if Mom already knew she was back in town.

Mom hugged her when she walked inside, obviously not surprised but happy she was there.

"Hank told you I was back," Holly said.

"No, Hank's not even here right now. I saw your things moved into your room when I got back."

"You're not supposed to be climbing stairs yet," Holly chided.

"I'm progressing faster than you realize. It's good exercise for me," Mom said enthusiastically. "Now, sit down and tell me what's happening with you."

Holly and Mom sat at the kitchen table, and Holly eagerly explained her plans for the future. She told her she was going to look for a job near Sandalwood, possibly in Columbus. She would live at the house until she passed the bar. Holly also told her that she and Andrew were back together, but explained how things were different now.

Holly thought Mom would be upset, fearing that her relationship with Andrew would once again end in disaster. But she surprised her.

"It sounds like you two are finally on the right track."

"Really?" Holly said excitedly.

"Yes, really. A few things have happened here since you were in Chicago," Mom said.

"Is anything wrong?" Holly asked quickly.

"I don't think so. I actually think it's a good thing," Mom answered. "I sold the restaurant."

Holly's jaw dropped, and she was momentarily without words. "Mom," she finally said. "You owned that restaurant for over twenty years. That was you and Dad's life's work."

Mom smiled. "You're right. It was a big part of our lives. But your dad is gone now, and that part of my life is over. To be honest, your dad and I had been talking about it for the last few months."

"But Gary and Eileen can help run it. What are they going to do without the restaurant? Or Mike and all the other employees?"

"Gary and Eileen are the ones who bought it. All the employees will stay, and everything will continue as it was. It's time for me to move on to a new chapter in my life."

"I guess that's true for everyone in this family," Holly said.

"I'm giving the money I got from the restaurant to you and Hank. It will help both of you to start over."

"Mom, you need that money for yourself."

Mom shook her head. "I got plenty of money from the insurance company after the accident. I'll be more than okay."

"I've got one question," Holly said.

"What's that?" Mom asked.

"Did Hank decide to stay in Sandalwood before or after you told him he was getting half the proceeds from the diner?"

"Neither. I haven't told him yet."

"Really?" Holly said. She was more impressed with her brother than she had been in years. "So he decided to come home, take an honest job, and clean his life up all on his own."

"Not all on his own. Do you know how many years your dad and I have been praying for him to straighten his life out?"

"I hope there were a few prayers in there for me, too," Holly said.

"Always," Mom said. "Is there something in particular that needs praying about?" she said, raising a suspicious eyebrow.

Holly smiled and headed upstairs to do some studying.

***

That evening, while Mom was fixing dinner, Hank was out looking for a job, and Holly was relaxing on the porch, Andrew pulled into the drive. Holly glanced at her phone, checking the time. She couldn't believe it was after five. She'd lost track of the time since coming downstairs for a break after studying. She was already easing into a more slow-paced lifestyle.

"Hey, you," he said, getting out of the car and coming up to the porch. Andrew had texted earlier and said he might stop by if he could get off work in time for dinner.

"You got everything taken care of earlier than you thought?" Holly said as she slowly pushed the porch swing.

"Yeah, it doesn't get too crazy busy until January." He sat down next to her and gently rested his arm around her shoulders.

She looked up at the rising moon and sighed. "Hard to believe it's almost Thanksgiving," she said.

"I have only one more thing to say about the past before we both move on to the future," he said softly. "I'm sorry we wasted eight years finding each other again."

"They weren't wasted," Holly insisted. "I think we each had to make our way in the world and find out who we were before we were ready to really be together."

Andrew smiled. "I suppose you're right about that. And it's going to be that much sweeter after everything we've been through."

Holly threw her arms around Andrew. "We have a lot to be thankful for this year."

About the author

Stasia Diann

Besides *Holly's Hometown Heartache*, Stasia Diann has also written several children's novels under her pen name, Staz. All of her books are human-written and family-friendly.

Middle grade and young adult novels written by Staz include *Mrs. Mercutrode*, *The Last Drop*, *Almost Normal*, *The Burning Tree*, and

Ginger. You can find her children's books on the website stazbooks.com and Christian romance books on stasiaromance.carrd.co.